Vortex

A CODE RED ADVENTURE

CHRIS RYAN

DOUBLEDAY

VORTEX
A DOUBLEDAY BOOK 978 0 385 61295 1
TRADE PAPERBACK 978 0 385 61296 8

Published in Great Britain by Doubleday,
an imprint of Random House Children's Books
A Random House Group Company

This edition published 2008

1 3 5 7 9 10 8 6 4 2

Mixed Sources
Product group from well-managed
forests and other controlled sources
www.fsc.org   Cert no. TT-COC-2139
© 1996 Forest Stewardship Council
FSC

Set in 13.5/17.5 pt Garamond by
Falcon Oast Graphic Art Ltd.

RANDOM HOUSE CHILDREN'S BOOKS
61–63 Uxbridge Road, London W5 5SA

www.**kids**at**random**house.co.uk
www.rbooks.co.uk

Addresses for companies within The Random House Group Limited can be found at:
www.randomhouse.co.uk/offices.htm

THE RANDOM HOUSE GROUP Limited Reg. No. 954009

A CIP catalogue record for this book is available from the British Library.

Printed in the UK by Clays Ltd, Bungay, Suffolk

Vortex

www.**rbooks**.co.uk

A CODE RED ADVENTURE

Location:

*on the borders
of Cumbria and
Northumberland,
the United
Kingdom*

Prologue

1957. A secret location somewhere in England. Dawn.

He was far more ruthless and efficient than any weapon man could devise. And there was silence, high above the ground, as he watched patiently, waited to go in for the kill. His prey was down there – a long way down – but his eyes were keen and he was hungry.

The grey feathers of the male hen harrier made him look more like a ghost than a real bird as he drifted eerily against the steely light of the dawn sky. He glided effortlessly, his wings fixed in a shallow V-shape as, with the skill of a true hunter, he stalked his unsuspecting prey, low over the ground, only a few metres above the small rodent that would have run had it only known what was about to happen.

And when the moment came, the rodent barely even had time to whimper.

The hen harrier pounced with lightning speed, his talons carrying his suddenly motionless prey high into the sky. All need for secrecy gone, he let out his distinctive cry, a shrill, repetitive trilling that echoed through the crystal morning air. In response, there came a second cry – a female this time – and as if those two bird calls had been a signal for something, the air was suddenly filled with the kaleidoscope sounds of the dawn chorus. But it was the call of the hen harrier that was most distinctive of all.

The bird came to rest in a patch of tall grass just by a dirt track seldom used by people. Hidden. Protected. Safe from the ravenous eyes of other predators, and the thoughtless, dangerous movements of man.

As he fed, however, his sharp ears became aware of another noise. A strange noise. Not the dawn chorus, but something else: a low-pitched rumble, in the distance, but getting nearer. His head twitched in the direction of the noise, and he appeared for a moment to be listening intently as the sound grew louder. Suddenly the hen harrier grabbed his prey firmly in his talons once more and took again to the skies. By the time the truck passed the grassy patch where he had been, the bird was long gone.

It was a military vehicle – a three-ton general service

truck left over from the war. Its army-green paint had started to peel and rust in places, but its wheels were chunky and serviceable and the khaki canopy over the back fully intact. The men who drove in it were not soldiers, however: they wore slightly frayed suits, one dark green, the other brown, with white shirts and thin ties. The man in the passenger seat was young and bespectacled; the driver was older and balding. Both were pale, and neither of them spoke a word to each other. They just looked straight ahead as their bodies shook in time with the movement of the truck over the bumpy road.

'Easy,' the younger man said finally as the truck motored over a particularly treacherous patch of ground. 'Let's not shake him up any more than we have to.'

His colleague momentarily glanced over his shoulder, as though he might be able to see through the back of the cab and into the canopied trailer behind them. But of course he couldn't and he just continued to drive in silence, though a little slower now.

Up ahead a small hut came into view. It had been constructed from concrete, and it looked new. Even the metal door – a familiar green colour – seemed to have been recently painted. The truck came to a halt just outside, and as the animal growl of the diesel engine faded to nothing, the ears of the two men were filled with another sound. It was coming from the trailer and it was unmistakable.

It was the sound of a man screaming.

They sat there for a moment, the muffled shouts filling their ears. 'Please, let me out! Please, don't do this! *You don't have to do this!*'

The younger man breathed in deeply and you could hear his breath shaking.

'It's the best thing for him, Lucian,' his colleague said quietly. 'The right thing. You do understand that, don't you? You do agree? If he messes everything up, who knows what they'll do to him?'

Lucian nodded grimly. 'It's OK,' he said. 'You won't get any trouble from me.'

'Good.' The older man nodded with satisfaction. 'We'll open up first, then get him out.'

Lucian climbed down from the cab and walked with his colleague towards the door. It was a relief to get away from the screaming. What was about to happen was not going to be nice. Not nice at all. But sometimes you had to think of the greater good. Their research was too important to be compromised by one man, even if that man did happen to be his brother. And like his friend had said, it was for his own benefit.

With the metal door unlocked, they walked into the hut.

Inside it was empty – concrete walls, concrete floor.

But at the far end, against one of the walls, there was a wooden trap door. The older man unlocked it with a large key, then pulled it up. He disappeared momentarily down a flight of steps, then Lucian saw light flood out of the opening and his friend reappeared. He gave Lucian a determined nod, and the two of them returned to the car.

The screaming had stopped now, and when the older man opened the back of the truck, Lucian could see why. His brother was still there of course, hook-nosed and floppy-haired, his bright green eyes flashing in the darkness and his hands tied tightly behind his back; but now he was cowering in the corner of the truck, clearly terrified by the fact that they had come to a standstill. Lucian looked him straight in the eye.

'Please,' his brother whispered, as though all the fight had been knocked out of him. 'Please don't do this. *I'm your brother.*'

Lucian shook his head. This was for his brother's own good, he told himself yet again.

The older man jumped up into the cab of the truck and roughly tugged at the captive's arm. Limply, Lucian's brother stumbled along with him, and when he was thrown from the trailer, he fell to the ground like a puppet with no strings. Lucian and his colleague took one bound arm each and dragged him, whimpering, into the hut and down the stairs.

Lucian had never been down here before, but he knew of its reputation of course. This was where the experiments were done. By the light of the solitary yellow light bulb hanging from the ceiling he could see in the centre of the room a heavy metal chair, bolted firmly to the ground. The walls were covered with locked cabinets, and an empty metal trolley stood by the chair.

The older man roughly untied Lucian's brother. As if given a new lease of life by the freedom of his wrists, he started flailing uncontrollably, hitting out at his captors as they firmly, forcibly restrained him and pushed him into the chair. Lucian kept him sitting while the other man gagged his mouth.

'Is that really necessary?' Lucian asked.

'I'm afraid so,' his colleague replied. 'We've had instances where subjects have bit into their tongues. It's not a pretty sight.'

The gag did not stop the man from starting to scream again, however, and Lucian did his best to ignore the pitiful wails as he watched his colleague make a large rip in the shirt around his brother's upper arm, then turn and unlock a cupboard on the wall. He brought out a bottle filled with a clear liquid, and a hypodermic needle.

'Lysergic acid diethylamide,' he observed shortly, though he needn't have.

Lucian knew perfectly well what it was.

At the sight of the needle, however, his brother had fallen silent and was now shaking violently.

'Will he remember anything?' Lucian asked.

'Bits and pieces,' the older man replied. 'He'll need a few treatments like this, but at the end of it he'll be very confused. With hallucinations. Probably for the rest of his life.'

He placed the bottle on the table, opened it, and inserted the syringe.

'The kind of doses we're going to give him will be enough to induce frequent psychotic episodes, especially as his mental health is frail at the moment.' He smiled. 'The upshot is,' he added, 'that nobody's going to believe a word your brother tells them. They'll think he's a lunatic. With a bit of luck, anything he tries to tell them about this place will be laughed off as the ravings of a madman. But I should warn you – the first treatment is always the most traumatic.'

Lucian looked down at his brother, seeing the fear in his eyes. Fear like he had never seen before. 'It's best this way,' he told his brother in a flat tone of voice, before watching what happened next with a kind of grisly fascination.

The metal of the needle glistened in the bright over-head light, and the patient started to hyperventilate as the older man approached him implacably.

He only screamed once, but that scream lasted from the moment the needle slid into his arm until after the clear fluid had been slowly and carefully pumped into his system. Lucian had heard people talk of blood-curdling screams before, but had never quite known what the phrase meant. He knew now. His veins turned to ice and his limbs felt heavy on his body.

It's for his own good, he told himself, as he gazed dispassionately down on the shuddering body of his brother and stared as those piercing green eyes that had watched him ever since he was a child widened suddenly in a ghastly, almost inhuman stare.

The needle was pulled out of the man's arm, and he screamed again – not for as long this time, but just as loud. Still, Lucian knew that the walls of this place were thick. He doubted anyone would be able to hear the noise his brother was making.

And he was right.

As the sun continued to rise outside the hut, there was nothing to suggest what was going on below ground. Just the usual sound of the dawn chorus, and the ghostly sight of another hen harrier soaring high above the trees.

Chapter One

Fifty years later

Ben Tracey was bored.

Only a couple of weeks ago, when he had been stuck in a remote part of Africa in circumstances that, frankly, he wouldn't care to repeat, he'd have given anything to be back in rainy, grey Macclesfield. But now he was here, he found the four walls of his bedroom closing in on him, and his mood was as grim as the incessant and unseasonable rain that had been hammering against the windowpane for three days now, although it seemed much longer. The remainder of the summer holidays seemed to stretch endlessly before him: it would almost be a relief, he thought to himself more than once, to get back to school.

He could always phone round a few friends, of

course, see what everybody was up to, maybe even go out; but something stopped him from doing that. He was a bit embarrassed to admit it, even to himself, but since his adventures in London, Adelaide and the Democratic Republic of the Congo, the pursuits and interests of his friends had seemed a bit . . . he didn't want to use the word *childish*, but he supposed that was it. More than that, he was beginning to get a bit paranoid. Stuff just seemed to happen to Ben Tracey. He had a knack of being in the wrong place at the wrong time, and it was a miracle he'd come through it all unscathed. He wasn't the type to brag about it, though, and none of his friends really knew what he'd been up against. They probably wouldn't believe him in any case, so he just kept quiet about it all and hoped his days of finding himself in mortal danger were at an end.

It didn't have to be *quite* this dull, though, did it? he thought to himself as he continued to watch the rain-drops slide down the window.

He was woken from his daydream by a beeping sound. On the table in his bedroom, hidden under a mess of old magazines and T-shirts that should prob-ably have found their way into the dirty-washing basket, was his new PDA – a present from his dad. 'For everything you've done,' Russell had said awkwardly, shaking Ben's hand in a grown-up kind of way as though they were work colleagues rather than father and son. Ben had mumbled a slightly embarrassed word of thanks, but once he'd opened the package, he was actually pretty excited. Say what you like about his dad, but as a scientist he was a bit like a teenager when it came to the latest electronic gadgets, and the device Ben held in his hand was pretty neat. He'd filled a good deal of time working his way around it over the past few days, and now he rummaged around on his messy table to find the palm-sized computer.

It was an email, he saw, as he tapped his finger to the screen, and his face lightened up into a broad smile when he saw who it was from: Annie, his cousin. Actually, she was his second cousin, or was it his cousin once removed? He'd forgotten, if he ever even knew, but it was always good to hear from her.

Plenty of people thought Annie was a bit weird. Truth to tell, she *was* a bit weird – Ben smiled to himself – but that didn't mean she wasn't good company. To look at her you'd think she was just another ordinary teenage girl: quite pretty, fashionably dressed; but there was a lot more to Annie than met the eye.

Her father, James Macpherson, was an air commodore in the RAF. Ben had seen him a number of times in his military uniform, and his jacket was practically plastered in colourful decorations for bravery. He'd been all over the world with his job, and still spent more time away from home than he did with his family. Annie adored him – idolized him, even – and as a result she was obsessed with all things military. She could tell you the spec of any plane you cared to show her, she knew more about guns than anybody Ben had ever met, and she was, for her age, an expert at tae kwon do. It was an extremely bad idea to try and patronize Annie by asking her a girlie question about her make-up – you were likely to end up groaning on the floor in agony after receiving a well-placed kick in the knee.

Ben opened up the email. Like Annie, it was curt and to the point:

GOING BIRD-WATCHING FOR A COUPLE OF DAYS. FANCY COMING ALONG?
ANNIE

That was another thing about Annie. Her hobbies were her hobbies – it didn't matter to her one bit that some girls her age would have scorned the idea of going bird-watching. She'd been an avid birder for as long as Ben could remember, and had been trying to get him to join her for ages. There had always been some reason why he couldn't, but now he thought that a few days in Annie's company was just what he needed. Moreover, it would get him out of the house and fill his time more productively than moping around here.

And besides, it was just a bird-watching trip. They weren't heading into any major natural catastrophes; they weren't heading into any dangerous, war-torn corners of the world. It was a bird-watching trip, plain and simple. Just him, Annie and a couple of pairs of binoculars.

You couldn't get much safer than that, could you?

The old man didn't really know where he was. He knew it was an institution, of course, but it could have been anywhere in the country. Perhaps it was a week ago that they'd moved him here, perhaps a month or even a year. Time had long since ceased to mean much to him.

He sat in the common room, keeping himself to himself. How he loathed this place: the way all the furniture was firmly screwed to the floor, the antiseptic smell. His face was firmly locked into a position that expressed all that loathing, his lip curled and the steeliness around his green eyes interrupted only by the occasional twitch of his left cheek – a nervous tic that had been with him since he was a young man. But he couldn't stay in his room all day. 'Enough to drive you mad,' he would joke in his high-pitched voice to the nurses, who always seemed uncomfortable with his sense of humour.

The television was blaring in the corner, and five or

six other inmates were staring at it intently. Everyone else called them patients, of course, but he preferred to think of them as inmates, because that's what they were. They all wore the same clothes as him – plain trousers, T-shirts and slip-on shoes. No belts, no shoelaces, nothing that could be used to harm themselves or others. None of them were taking in a single word that was being said on the television – the old man could tell that much from the look on their faces.

Days just merged into one for him now. He would be woken at seven o'clock with his daily cocktail of medicines – anti-psychotics, anti-depressants, anti-this, anti-that – then left to his own devices. Most days he would read in the morning – scientific journals from the hospital library. His reading was slow these days, and not just because of his eyesight, but he liked to keep abreast of things. Somehow it made him feel as if his life was not being wasted. He had long since grown used to the unpleasant hospital food that was served at lunch time, and he would eat what he was given enthusiastically, knowing that he had to keep his strength up. In the afternoon he would sleep – the drugs made him tired; sometimes he would have meetings with the doctors, little more than kids to his old eyes, and answer the same questions that he had been answering for so many years.

All this was assuming he was not in the middle of

what they politely referred to as an 'episode'. When he was having an episode, everything was different. Every*one* was different.

One of the inmates started shouting – a hoarse, hollow bark that would have been alarming had such sounds not been commonplace around here. Almost immediately a female nurse hurried into the common room to check on him. She had a friendly face – open and clear – and she put her clipboard and security card down on the table beside her as she wrapped an arm around the distressed inmate and spoke to him with calm, soothing words. Her patient started murmuring. The old man couldn't hear what he was saying, but soon the nurse seemed satisfied that she had settled him. She picked up her clipboard and left the room.

It took a few moments for the old man to realize what he was seeing. The nurse's security badge had fallen to the floor, and she had left without picking it up.

His limbs suddenly froze with adrenaline. His green eyes flickered around: had anyone been looking at him, they might have thought he appeared shifty. But nobody *was* looking at him – they were all distracted by the blare of the television.

He had to move quickly, that much he knew. He had escaped once before, many years ago and out of a place very different from this. Things had been different then. Less enlightened. When they finally caught him, he had been brutally restrained and dealt with severely. It had blunted his taste for freedom considerably. But lately he had been dreaming of trying again. He was old. He had been assessed as unlikely ever to be suitable for care in the community and so, if he wanted to live a little of his life on the outside now, he would have to take risks. But risks don't seem that risky when you have nothing to lose.

This was what he had been waiting for. An opportunity.

He stood up and sidled over to the inmate the nurse had been looking after. As he did so, he started to prepare himself to make small talk, but there was no need: the inmate did not seem to notice him as he bent down and slowly picked up the string with the nurse's card on it. Hiding it up his sleeve, he shuffled out of the common room.

It was busy in the corridor. He would have preferred to wait for a quieter time of day, but he knew that the nurse would soon realize she had forgotten her badge; when she realized it was missing, the whole hospital would be shut down. He was a familiar enough face, though, to be walking around, so nobody paid him any attention as he made his way towards the exit.

Suddenly he heard a voice. 'Everything all right, Joseph?' it said in a pronounced Cornish accent.

Joseph stopped still, then turned, very slowly, to see the smiling face of one of the young doctors who insisted on asking him foolish questions about 'how he was feeling'. He stared at the doctor for a moment, feeling his face twitching involuntarily. 'Everything's all right, Doctor,' he said finally. 'Everything's all right. Yes.' His head continued to nod as he spoke, and his fingers moved up to flick his floppy hair out of his eyes.

'Good,' the doctor replied, his face concerned. He stepped back a pace or two, his eyes narrowing slightly, before turning and walking off. Joseph stood still, watching him until he turned round a corner out of sight. Then he continued on his way.

There was a receptionist at the exit – a young man whom he did not recognize – but no security guard, he was relieved to see. Joseph stood a little distance away, watching him carefully. He was too old to run, and that would only have drawn attention to him anyway, but he knew he only needed the receptionist to be distracted for a few moments to give him his chance. He felt his bony hands shaking with anticipation.

The moment came soon enough.

The phone rang, and the young man's face lit up. Clearly it was a personal call – a girlfriend, maybe. The phone firmly pressed to his ear, he sat back in his swivel chair and spun round. Joseph didn't waste a second. He strode to the door and swiped the nurse's security card.

The door slid open. He took a deep breath and, without looking back, stepped out into the main body of the hospital.

It was even more crowded here, and he went entirely unnoticed. By the time the alarm was raised in the psychiatric wing and the doors were locked down, he was out of the hospital, walking calmly and slowly down the road, an unknowable look in his eyes.

Chapter Two

Later that afternoon, Ben was jumping off a bus at the end of Annie's street. The rain had let up a bit, but there was still a grey drizzle and he was glad of the hood on his raincoat as he hurried down the road and knocked on the door of her parents' large, imposing house. A dog started to bark, and soon the door was opened by Annie's mum, a harassed-looking woman in the middle of a telephone conversation. 'She's upstairs,' she mouthed to Ben, pointing to the stairs. 'In her room.'

Ben smiled, stroked the ears of the Alsatian that was enthusiastically sniffing his legs, then went up to find Annie.

'Hi, An—' he started to say, but stopped when he saw her.

Annie was eccentric, to say the least, but he wasn't quite prepared for this. She was in the middle of her room, standing on one leg on top of a plastic storage box with a pair of woollen tights wrapped round her head as a blindfold. Both arms were raised in the air as she stood perfectly still, like a statue.

'Come in!' she said brightly.

'Er, right.' Ben edged round her and sat on the edge of her bed, not quite knowing if it would be rude to chat. 'It's me – Ben,' he offered finally.

'How's things?' Annie asked, still barely moving.

'Fine.'

He sat there in silence for a moment, looking awkwardly round the room. It wasn't a typical girl's room: there was a dressing table with various pots and potions that were a mystery to Ben, but on the wall there were pictures cut out from military magazines. Ben recognized a Typhoon F1 on one wall, and a jump jet on another. There was also a huge poster of British birds, as well as a photograph of her dad in full RAF regalia. Ben looked at the pictures for a while before turning his attention back to Annie.

'You going to be like that for a long time?' he asked eventually. 'Because I can always come back.'

Annie lowered one of her hands and removed the tights from around her eyes. Then she looked down at herself and managed to seem a bit surprised at the position she was in. 'Sorry,' she said whimsically, before jumping down off the box and kissing Ben lightly on the cheek. 'Just practising. You sort of get into it.'

'I thought tae kwon do was all, you know, beating people up and stuff.'

Annie gave him a cross look. 'Who do you think I am, Ben? A Teenage Mutant Ninja thingy?' Ben thought she sounded a bit more scornful than she needed to. 'I do tae kwon do because it's healthy, OK?'

Ben nodded, doing his best not to look amused. He felt quite sure that Annie had not neglected the martial arts side of her 'exercise' regime, but he didn't fancy being at the receiving end of it, so he kept quiet as he watched her put the plastic box away.

'So,' he said to break the silence, 'where are we going?'

Annie's face lit up as she practically skipped to her bookcase and brought down an ordnance survey map. She indicated that Ben should sit down with her on the floor, then spread the map open in front of them, and pointed at the area just west of the Northumbria National Park. 'Here,' she told him. 'There's a youth hostel we can stay at, and it's dead close to the area where we can find what we're looking for.'

'Right,' Ben said vaguely. 'We looking for something in particular, then?'

'Well, we're not out to spot pigeons, Ben,' Annie told him as she jumped up and selected something else from her bookcase – a magazine this time. Ben saw the blue

21

and white logo of the RSPB on the front. She flicked through until she came across the page she wanted, then handed it to Ben. 'Hen harrier,' she said shortly. 'Very rare. We'll be lucky to find them.'

Ben looked at the pages. There were pictures of two birds – a male and a female, the text told him. The female was brown, and stared out of the picture with a certain ferocity, her beady eyes seeming to bore straight into Ben, her hooked beak sharp and threatening. The male did not appear so aggressive, but seemed no less mysterious to Ben. He was grey – like the ghost of a bird, he thought – and had a striking nobility about him.

'They're amazing,' he said quietly.

Annie nodded soberly. 'They are,' she said.

'Why are they so rare?'

'Because they're carnivorous,' she explained.

Ben looked confused. 'I don't understand. Wouldn't that make them stronger – top of the food chain and all that?'

Annie was still gazing at the magazine on Ben's lap. She reached out and touched the picture of the male hen harrier almost wistfully. 'There's not much they can do about guns, though.'

'Guns?' Ben was shocked. 'Who would want to shoot them?'

'Gamekeepers,' Annie explained. She had a sad kind

of smile on her face. 'You see, the hen harrier is a natural predator of grouse. So some gamekeepers have been breaking the law by shooting harriers to keep their grouse stocks up so that people can then pay to shoot the grouse. We humans can do some pretty dumb things sometimes. It's gone on for years. Anyway, it's got really bad lately. There's only about seven hundred and fifty breeding pairs in the whole of the United Kingdom – and the English population is tiny. Only ten pairs in 2004, and my magazine says that there were only fifteen successful nests this year. That makes hen harriers really rare.'

Ben didn't know much about these things, but fifteen nests sounded like the birds were seriously in danger of being wiped out.

'The area where we're going is one of the few spots in the country where you can still see them, and now's the right time of year. If we see one, we need to make a detailed description of it and report it to the RSPB – they keep tabs on things like this because the birds are so rare. I can't promise we'll have any luck, but—'

'It's OK,' Ben interrupted. 'It'll just be nice to get away.' He glanced slightly glumly out of Annie's bedroom window at the persistent drizzle. 'Hope the weather clears up, though.'

'Yeah,' Annie replied, 'because the thing is, we'll probably die if we get wet, won't we?' She elbowed Ben playfully but – he thought – a bit sharply in the ribs. 'You're not going to wimp out on me because of a few drops of water, are you?'

Ben smiled, and he thought back momentarily to the floods in London and the torrential rains in the Congo.

'No,' he said quietly, 'I'm OK with a bit of rain. You don't have to worry about that.' And he went back to staring at the picture of the hen harrier, and wondering if they might be lucky enough to catch sight of one in real life.

Inspector Tim Matthews was a good deal younger than the clinical psychiatrist sitting opposite, but that didn't stop him looking at the guy with an expression of incredulity.

'You're trying to tell me that he just walked out?'

Dr Hopkinson raised his hands in the air and shrugged slightly. 'I know, it doesn't sound good, but there we have it,' he conceded. 'I guess we took our eye off the ball for a moment.'

The room in which they were sitting – Dr Hopkinson's study – was cluttered with files, papers and well-thumbed medical books.

'How did it happen? I thought this place was meant to be secure.'

'It is,' Dr Hopkinson replied. 'The only way in and out is using swipe cards, and they're only given to authorized personnel. Unfortunately, one of our nurses mislaid hers when she was attending to a patient, and our man was able to grab it and leave without being noticed. She's getting an official warning as we speak, but the truth is that it was just a human error.'

The policeman sighed and pulled a notebook out of his jacket. 'All right then,' he said in a resigned tone of voice. 'You'd better tell me what you know about him.'

Hopkinson looked seriously at him. 'You do understand, officer, that this is confidential. As his doctor, I have a certain duty towards my patients.'

'All we want to do is find him, Doctor Hopkinson.'

The doctor nodded, and placed his fingers together. 'His name is Joseph Sinclair. He's been sectioned under the Mental Health Act for the past twenty-five years – since the act was established, in fact. Before that, he was in a number of institutions. The records are a bit vague.' He smiled apologetically. 'I'm afraid the medical profession has not always been quite as enlightened in these matters as we are now.'

'Any family?'

'He's mentioned a brother, but not in kindly terms. Certainly there's no contact – he hasn't had a visitor for as long as I've been his doctor.'

The policeman nodded. 'What's wrong with him?' he asked.

'A classic case of paranoid schizophrenia,' Dr

Hopkinson replied. 'Textbook stuff, really – voices in his head, government conspiracies, men in black out to get him. He's convinced that his mental illness derives from treatments he was given by a government agency when he was a young man. It's a very common delusion. Most of the time he keeps quiet about it, but now and then he exhibits acute psychotic episodes: when that happens, we have to keep him restrained, for his own good and that of others.'

Inspector Matthews looked sharply at him. 'Violent tendencies?'

Dr Hopkinson thought about that for a moment. 'Difficult to say,' he answered finally, 'because we never let it get that far. But with this kind of psychosis, you can never count it out. That's why he's been assessed as unsuitable for any form of community care – he needs to be in a secure institution like ours, for his own good. And now he's out there without his medicines – a few days like that and his symptoms *are* very likely to escalate.'

'OK. Do you have a picture of him?'

The psychiatrist opened a file in front of him and withdrew a photograph. 'This was taken about three years ago,' he said. 'He hasn't changed much since.'

Inspector Matthews looked at the picture. The man who stared back out at him had a hooked nose and grey floppy hair. But it was his eyes that stood out the most. Piercing, green, beady almost – like a hawk. There was something about them that made him feel distinctly uncomfortable. 'How old is he?' the policeman asked quietly.

'Seventy-one, but fit for his age.'

'Still,' Inspector Matthews replied, 'he's an old man. We'll alert the local police forces and search the surrounding area. I can't imagine he'll have it in him to get too far.'

But Dr Hopkinson didn't seem so convinced. 'Inspector Matthews,' he said politely, 'I hope you don't think I'm trying to tell you your job, but—' He hesitated.

'Go on, Doctor,' the policeman encouraged.

'Don't underestimate Joseph Sinclair. He's old, and his mental health is frail. But he's not stupid – I've had enough conversations with him to establish that. He has a scientific mind, he's a voracious reader and he's no fool.'

'What are you trying to tell me, Doctor?'

Dr Hopkinson looked away for a moment. 'I don't know,' he replied. 'Just don't expect to find him sitting in a field somewhere talking to the daisies. Just because he suffers from psychosis, it doesn't mean he can't merge into society perfectly easily.'

The policeman nodded. 'Point taken,' he said. 'In

the meantime, you'd better hope the press don't get hold of this – they'd have a field day.'

Dr Hopkinson smiled. 'I'm concerned about my patients,' he said honestly. 'Not chattering journalists.'

He watched as the policeman closed his notebook, put it away and stood up to leave. 'Thank you, Doctor Hopkinson,' he said. 'I'll be in touch.' Inspector Matthews made to leave, but before he reached the door he stopped and turned to look back at the doctor. 'Just one other thing,' he said, a certain hesitation in his voice.

'Of course,' the doctor replied.

'If this guy is as sharp as you say, all the stuff about government conspiracies and the like – has anyone actually checked that it isn't *true*?' He seemed a bit embarrassed to be asking the question.

Dr Hopkinson stood up. 'Officer!' he exclaimed. 'I didn't have you down as a conspiracy theorist.' Suddenly his face became more serious as he stared directly at the policeman. 'Believe me,' he said clearly, 'we don't lightly section people. I've been in this job for twenty years now. If I had a pound for every time I heard a paranoid schizophrenic tell me there was a government conspiracy to silence them, I promise you, I'd be a rich man. Joseph Sinclair is smart, but he's delusional. He needs to be back here, where we can look after him.'

The policeman appeared chastened, even slightly embarrassed to have asked the question. 'Of course, Doctor,' he said politely, then left the room, closing the door firmly behind him.

Chapter Three

Haltwhistle Station was like a ghost town when they arrived.

It had been a five-hour train journey from Macclesfield to the sleepy rural village that claimed to be the exact geographical centre of the country but which seemed to Ben to be the end of the earth. Ben had spent some of the time being instructed in ornithological matters by Annie. She made, he thought, a strange sight, dressed in army surplus combat trousers and boots as she pored over pictures of obscure British birds, but that was her through and through. Ben was also dressed in sturdy outdoor gear, and was glad of it: the rain had let up, but each time they changed train, first at Manchester, then Lancaster and finally onto an elderly, two-carriage boneshaker at Carlisle, the air seemed to grow damper. He could hardly believe it was late summer.

On the last train they fell into a comfortable silence. Ben picked up a newspaper that somebody had left lying around and flicked through it. One of the main stories grabbed his interest. NORTH KOREA AGREES NUCLEAR STEPDOWN said the headline. He read further: *North Korea has agreed to disable its principal nuclear reactor, and to submit details to the West of its nuclear programme in a move that is widely seen as a peace overture from the totalitarian regime of this stricken country.'* He handed the newspaper to Annie and tapped the article. 'Looks like your dad might be out of a job if peace keeps breaking out everywhere,' he said archly.

Annie glanced at the article. 'Hardly,' she said. 'There's always some regime out there that thinks it's OK to start killing people. If it's not the North Koreans, it'll only be someone else.'

'I suppose you're right,' Ben agreed glumly, taking the paper back and continuing to flick through it.

When the time finally came to disembark for the last time, they lugged their rucksacks off the train with only a handful of other passengers, and then found the bus stop, a little way from the slate-roofed ticket office, where they waited for their bus to the youth hostel. Evening was drawing in now, and the place where they stood was practically deserted. It had already been a long day, and Ben and Annie stood in silence as they waited for the bus that didn't seem to want to come.

It was only gradually that the feeling came over Ben. It was a curious sensation, a bit like pins and needles but not so acute. The feeling of being watched. He looked around him, and at first could see nobody. But then he looked back towards the train station. An arched bridge connected the two platforms, and standing on top of it, silhouetted ghost-like against the dusk sky, was a figure. Something about him chilled Ben's blood.

The figure stood perfectly motionless, and Ben found himself squinting his eyes to try and make out his features more clearly. He was too far away, though, and the light was not good enough. Gently he nudged Annie.

'What?' she asked, tiredness showing in her voice.

Ben didn't say anything – he just nodded in the direction of the figure. Normally he would have expected a sarcastic comment from his cousin, but not tonight. She too fell silent as she watched the silhouette, clearly as unnerved by it as Ben was, though neither was able to pinpoint quite why.

Ben bent down to his rucksack, opened it up and pulled out the pair of binoculars that Annie had lent him. He knew how rude it would be to use them to stare at somebody so close, but he couldn't stop himself: he just wanted to be able to look at the guy clearly, to dispel some of the uneasiness he was feeling. He put the binoculars to his eyes and adjusted the focus. Gradually the man came into view.

He was elderly, tall and thin and wore a shabby grey overcoat. His nose was hooked and his floppy hair seemed to fall over his face, though he made no attempt to brush it off. His left cheek occasionally twitched nervously, but it was the eyes that alarmed Ben most of all. They seemed constantly to flick off in different directions, nervously – panicked, even – and they gave the man's face a scary, disturbed demeanour. It did nothing to ease Ben's mind. What was he doing there, all alone? What was he searching for? Ben felt scared of him, yet transfixed. For a moment he wondered if the man intended to throw himself in front of the next train.

Suddenly, Ben felt a shock of ice run through him. The man was staring at him – staring *straight at him* – and his eyes had stopped darting around, though his face still twitched. How long they remained like that, Ben couldn't have said. Seconds probably, although it seemed like an age, and he watched in horror as the man's lip curled into what could only be described as a smile – but a smile with no humour.

Ben found himself almost hypnotized by the man's eyes, and it was only the sudden sound of the bus pulling up that made him lower the binoculars. Again the man appeared to him as no more than a silhouette in the distance.

The two cousins shuffled their rucksacks onto the bus, a rickety old thing that was empty apart from the driver, who silently took their fares, then they grabbed seats together at the back of the vehicle. As the bus pulled out, Ben glanced out of the window in the direction of the railway bridge. The old man was no longer there.

It was Annie who finally broke the silence. 'Why d'you look at him through the binoculars?' she asked.

Ben shrugged. 'Don't know,' he replied a bit defensively. 'I just had a weird feeling, that's all. Like he was watching us.'

'It's all right,' Annie replied. 'He gave me the spooks too.' She looked out of the window herself. 'It's pretty remote up here,' she observed. 'That's why it's good for bird-watching. Not too many people. If I was a bird, that's definitely what I'd want. People aren't good for wildlife – they always seem to manage to mess it up somehow.'

And with that melancholy observation, they both fell quiet again.

It was nearly an hour's bus ride, and for all that time Ben could not get the image of the old man out of his head. For some reason the hooked nose and the way those beady eyes had stared directly at him put him in mind of the picture of the female hen harrier from Annie's RSPB magazine – a ridiculous notion, he knew, but sometimes when you're scared you look for associations that aren't really there. He was glad when they arrived at the youth hostel as it meant he could focus his mind on something else.

The hostel was a large, grey-stone building, stark and imposing against the twilight sky. It was the only building for as far as the eye could see, which gave it a sinister look; yet it seemed at the same time to welcome them, with the lights beaming out of all the windows. As they lugged their heavy bags through the front door, a young man who seemed nice enough to Ben, if a bit over-friendly, directed them to their respective dormitories – sparse rooms with four sets of bunk beds each and only a couple of other guests occupying them. A quick snack from some of the food they had brought with them, and before long they were asleep in bed.

Tomorrow would be an early start.

Ben was awoken by the gentle vibration of his mobile – Annie, giving him their arranged alarm call. It was still dark outside and it seemed an effort for him to shake off the blanket of sleep, but they had arranged to leave the youth hostel before dawn in order to be out and about when the sun rose, and in a few minutes they were standing outside the hostel warmly dressed against the night-time cold in their outdoor gear. Each of them carried their rucksack on their back, but they were lighter today, filled only with the equipment that would be useful to them on their day's trek.

It felt good to be out of doors as dawn crept across the sky. Here, among the lanes and the fields, Ben felt miles from anywhere and anyone, and as the sky lit up, it made them all the more aware of the vastness of the landscape around them. It seemed impossible that only yesterday they had been in grey, suburban Macclesfield.

As they tramped through the fields, there were few sounds around them other than the noise of their walking boots squelching in the marshy ground. Annie held the ordnance survey map in a protective plastic covering and directed them confidently to the north-west with the aid of a small orienteering compass. 'There's an RAF base in this direction,' she explained quietly to Ben – something about the early-morning light encouraged them to speak in hushed whispers. 'It's called Spadeadam, and it's massive – over nine thousand acres. We can't cross over the boundary, but we can skirt around it. It's a good place for bird-watching.'

Ben raised an eyebrow. 'Really?' he asked mildly. 'I'd have thought it was the last place you'd see them – noisy planes flying overhead and everything.'

Annie shook her head. 'Spadeadam covers huge areas of marshland,' she explained. 'The RAF have to make sure they protect the wildlife around here, so loads of it has been left untouched as a perfect natural habitat. My dad was posted here once, years ago. He told me all about it.'

As they had been speaking, the air had gradually started to become filled with the throng of bird song, as though somebody had slowly been turning the volume up. Ben and Annie stopped still and looked in wonder around them as the empty canopy of air became flecked with the black silhouettes of myriad birds rising up from the marshy land. All their senses seemed to be filled with the sights and sounds of nature, and Ben quickly fumbled in his rucksack for his binoculars while Annie took out a waterproof blanket and spread it on the ground in front of them. They lay down on their fronts like snipers, and feasted their eyes on the display that was acting itself out before them.

Annie was an informative guide, seeming to see things Ben would never have noticed, and able to identify birds by the idiosyncratic swoop of their wings or their distinctive cries. She pointed out peregrine falcons, kestrels, skylarks and various small songbirds, all the while talking in a low, monotone voice that did little to hide her thrill at what she saw. It didn't take long for Ben to become infected with her enthusiasm, and after a while he started recognizing the birds for himself. He could have lain there all day watching them.

As the morning grew brighter, however, the initial frenzy of activity started to subdue and Annie suggested that they start walking, both to warm up a bit, and to continue their hunt for the elusive hen harrier. They packed up their things and moved on.

They hiked towards an area of woodland and skirted around the edge of it for an hour or so. They talked only infrequently, Annie occasionally pointing out something of interest, but otherwise both of them enjoying the peace and the solitude. Eventually, though, they found their path blocked by a fence made from evil-looking barbed wire.

'This must be the boundary to Spadeadam,' Annie observed, looking slightly wistfully over it and into the land beyond. 'We'd better not cross it.'

Ben followed her gaze. 'It just looks like open countryside,' he said. 'If you think we've got a better chance of spotting our bird there I expect there's some way we could get through the fence – if not here then somewhere else.'

Annie gave him a withering look. 'My dad's an air commodore,' she reminded him. 'Bit embarrassing if I'm caught trespassing round here, don't you think?'

'Oh, yeah.' Ben grinned at her. 'I guess you're right. Fancy some breakfast?' He pulled a couple of chocolate bars out of his rucksack and they ate them in silence before continuing their trek by following the perimeter fence westwards.

They spotted the occasional interesting bird throughout the morning, but nothing more than they had seen at dawn, and no sight of the hen harrier. By early afternoon, their feet were getting sore and the rucksacks heavy, so they agreed to turn round and head back to the hostel. On the way, they found themselves chatting to pass the time. 'You've got a real thing about the RAF, haven't you?' Ben asked Annie as he caught her looking over the Spadeadam perimeter yet again.

She smiled. 'You could say that. When I'm old enough, I'm going to join up.'

'Why? I mean, I know because of your dad and everything, but you're the first girl I've met who wants to be in the military.'

Annie didn't answer for a moment, but walked thoughtfully by Ben's side. 'People think being in the army is all guns and fighting, but it's not,' she said finally. 'You get to help people – people who really need it. When my dad was in the Gulf, he found two Iraqi children whose parents had both been put in prison. They were living on the streets. He was able to do something for them, make sure they got a roof over their heads and something to eat.' She flashed a quick grin at him. 'Plus you get all the guns and fighting on top of that.'

Ben laughed, but as he did so Annie suddenly interrupted him. 'Shhh,' she hissed, grabbing him firmly by his arm and using her other hand to point in the air. 'Look!'

Ben followed the direction of her finger. Two birds were flying over Spadeadam in the distance, performing an intricate aerial dance. 'Hen harrier,' Annie whispered; they both fell instinctively to their knees and put the binoculars that had been hanging round their necks up to their eyes. In rapt attention, they watched the birds somersault in the air.

'Look at the male,' Annie whispered. 'He's got something in his talons. Do you see?'

Ben strained his eyes and thought he could just make out what Annie was talking about.

'Yeah,' he said. 'I can.'

'Watch carefully,' she told him. 'They do this amazing thing. The male bird performs a sky dance and passes the food to the female in mid-air.'

Ben watched it happen, and found he was holding his breath in anticipation as he did so. The male swooped and dived and then, in one spectacular movement, they met and the food passed from one to the other. Ben couldn't help breaking into a grin as it happened. He turned to look at Annie, to see that she too was beaming with wonder.

It all happened so quickly after that.

The sound of a single gunshot echoed around the countryside. A flurry of birds rose up from the high grass of the marshland; but there was one bird that would never rise up again. The male hen harrier dropped from the air like a stone.

Annie gasped. As she did so, there was another gunshot and, with pinpoint accuracy, the female fell to earth.

The girl's binoculars remained pointed at the empty sky where the hen harriers had been flying only seconds before; but something urged Ben to scour the ground. Gunshots didn't come from nowhere, and he was determined to find out who had just shot down the birds. High grass suddenly filled his vision, and as he moved his head swiftly from side to side, flashes of sky and the distant forest replaced them momentarily, until finally he found what he was looking for.

The man must have been several hundred metres away, and as he came into Ben's field of vision he was breaking his shotgun and allowing two spent cartridges to fly out over his right shoulder. 'Look,' Ben whispered hoarsely.

'I see him,' Annie replied, and they both stared at the man as he turned and walked away. Neither of them said what was clearly obvious, but Ben knew beyond question that they were both thinking it.

The man who had just shot two rare hen harriers was

wearing the distinctive khaki uniform of an RAF combat soldier.

As he walked out of sight, Ben and Annie lowered their binoculars in unison. And then, as though the sky itself was mourning the horrible sight they had just witnessed, it started to rain.

Chapter Four

It was a long walk back, not just because of the rain but also because of a frosty silence between them. Annie seemed to have taken the death of the bird as a personal insult, and Ben felt that as he was the closest person to her at the time, he was at the receiving end of her prickly reaction.

It was early evening by the time they returned, their clothes saturated by the rain. Ben felt numb, not only from the wet but also from the strain of the last few hours. Annie hadn't spoken, but he could tell she felt the same too. They changed into some dry clothes, hung their wet walking gear in the hostel's boiler room, a cavernous, musty basement thick with the aroma of drying clothes, and then headed off to the common room together.

The common room was a cosy but slightly shabby

place. There were squashy old sofas that sank deep as you sat in them, and low coffee tables that had seen better days. A soft-drink vending machine hummed gently in the corner, and on one side there was a kettle and tea-making things. Ben made a cup of hot, sweet tea for them both, and they sat side by side on a sofa in a deserted corner of the room. Small groups of people sat together talking quietly; here and there was the occasional solitary guest, minding their own business. They were a mixed bunch – not many of them were particularly young, despite the fact that this was a youth hostel. Ben wasn't minded to make eye contact with many of his fellow guests – he felt subdued and not much like talking to anybody.

They were glad of the warmth of the room after the soaking they had received, but were halfway through their tea before either of them spoke. 'Pretty weird day, huh?' Ben offered. He knew it sounded stupid even as he said it.

'*Weird?*' Annie spat. 'Is that all you can say? It was horrible.' She slammed her tea down on the table in front of her, causing some of it to slosh over her hand.

'All right, Annie,' Ben snapped at her, suddenly infuriated by her attitude. 'It wasn't me that killed the birds, you know.'

She wiped her tea-moistened hand against her trousers in annoyance. 'No one *said* you killed the birds, Ben. I'm just saying it was horrible, all right?'

He took a deep breath and tried to calm himself down. 'You're right,' he said quietly. 'It *was* horrible.' Annie was clearly spoiling for an argument, and there was no point getting into one with her. 'Do you think we should tell someone? I mean, surely it's illegal, what we saw.'

His cousin shrugged. 'Yes, I suppose so. We can call the RSPB when we get back: they'd definitely want to know about stuff like this going on – shooting hen harriers is illegal, and it's important to notify the authorities. I just wish we could identify the guy who did it. He shouldn't be allowed to get away with this. He should be prosecuted.'

'I could contact my mum,' Ben offered, trying to raise Annie's mood a bit. 'As she's an environmental campaigner, I bet she'd know people who would take an interest in all this.'

'Yeah, I guess,' Annie replied sullenly.

'I just—' Ben hesitated because he knew that what he was about to say would touch a nerve. 'I just don't understand why the RAF would be involved. Why are they shooting rare birds? It doesn't make any sense.'

'*It's not the RAF,*' Annie said through gritted teeth. 'I know it's not. They go out of their way to look after the environment up at Spadeadam.'

Ben gave her an involuntarily sceptical look. He

knew what he'd seen, after all, and it had been Annie herself who had identified the guy's RAF combat dress.

'Don't look at me like that, Ben,' Annie warned him. 'I know you think I'm only saying this because of my dad, but I'm not. Think about it – there'd be an outcry if that amount of land was given over to military training without any regard for the environment whatsoever. There's some other explanation. There has to be.' She stood up, and Ben was alarmed to see tears filling her eyes. 'I'm going to bed,' she said. 'And tomorrow, we walk in a different direction. I never want to see Spadeadam again.'

As she stormed out of the room, Ben realized that the other occupants had all stopped talking and were staring at them. Slightly embarrassed, he sat down again and went back to contemplating his cup of tea. Despite the fact that half of him wanted to follow and have it out with her, he knew Annie well enough to realize that continuing the row now would be the worst thing to do, especially as he was pretty on edge himself. Stuff would be better in the morning, he hoped. Besides, he didn't blame her for being angry – he'd been as shocked as her when they saw the birds plummet to the earth, and like her he didn't feel any desire to head back towards Spadeadam.

'Spadeadam?'

Ben jumped. The voice seemed to have come out

of nowhere. He looked up sharply and couldn't see anyone – for a moment he wondered if he had been imagining it.

'Been up to Spadeadam, did she say? The girl? The girl who just left?' The words seemed to tumble nervously over themselves.

Ben realized the voice was coming from behind him. When he turned to look at its owner, however, he had to catch his breath.

He recognized him at once, of course. The long floppy hair; the hook nose; the piercing green eyes; the grey overcoat that he wore despite the fact that it was quite warm in the common room. The ghostly old man from the railway bridge the previous day did not look quite so sinister close up, but that did not stop him from being spooky. He did not take his wide eyes off Ben, and the tic on his face seemed metronomic, like clockwork. Ben found the sudden shock of his presence so surprising that he was unable to answer; he just watched mutely as the old man walked round and took a seat on the sofa next to him, his wild eyes fixed on him all the time.

'I was just going to go to bed,' Ben said uncomfortably, desperate to get away but not wanting to appear rude. At these close quarters the old man was distinctly fragrant – Ben wondered what he was wearing under his overcoat, and noticed that his slip-on shoes were soiled, the bottom of his thin trousers torn.

The old man acted as if he hadn't even heard him. When he spoke again, it was in a conspiratorial whisper. 'Strange things happening at Spadeadam,' he said, his accent a curious hybrid of dialects. 'Always have been, ever since I can remember, ever since Blue Streak.'

Ben shifted uncomfortably in his seat. 'What's Blue—?' he started to say, but the old man continued to talk as though Ben wasn't even there.

'They cover it all up, of course. Have to, don't they?' Suddenly his head twisted back over his shoulder as though he were looking for someone, or something, and his face started to twitch more frequently. He continued to look around, and his eyes even started darting up and down, as though he expected something to come at him from one of the top corners of the room.

Ben wanted to stand up and leave; but something about what the old man was saying had grabbed his attention. 'Cover what up?' he asked. 'What are you talking about?'

The old man seemed suddenly to remember that he was there. He turned his attention back to Ben, and slowly his lips curled into a grotesque mockery of a smile, displaying yellowing teeth with more gaps than there should have been. It was as though his face had forgotten what a smile looked like.

'Not a place for young 'uns, Spadeadam,' he whispered. 'Best to stay away.' The old man started looking up to the ceiling again.

This conversation was giving Ben a very uneasy feeling. Spadeadam was just an RAF base, wasn't it? There were plenty of them dotted around all over the country – what was so different about this one? Any other time, he would have dismissed this guy's comments as the ramblings of a crazy old man. Problem was, he seemed to be echoing all Ben's unspoken feelings about the place. Annie had been right – there had to be some sort of explanation for what they had seen earlier in the day. It was a long shot, but maybe this old man had the answer.

'Um . . . excuse me,' Ben asked politely, and the old man's eyes shot instantly back at him. 'Can I ask you a question – about Spadeadam, I mean?'

The old man didn't answer, but Ben assumed that his fixed stare was an agreement.

'We saw something earlier on, me and my friend. Two birds, being shot down by a guy in an RAF uniform.'

Suddenly the man grabbed Ben by the wrist. As Ben looked at his hand, pale and covered with prominent blue veins, he noticed that it was surprisingly strong. 'Rare breed, was it?' the man asked.

'Very rare,' Ben replied. 'One of the rarest.'

'Makes sense, doesn't it? Makes perfect sense.'

But it didn't make any kind of sense to Ben. 'Not really,' he started to say. But as he spoke, he sensed someone else approaching them. He looked up to see the friendly receptionist who had greeted them when they arrived the previous day. He was still smiling, but had a firm demeanour as he approached. The old man saw him too. Immediately he let go of Ben's arm and, as swiftly as a bird flying from a loud noise, he stood up straight and walked to the common-room door. Ben and the hostel worker watched him go, but before he left the room the old man turned round and fixed Ben with another of his piercing stares.

'Stay away from Spadeadam,' he called hoarsely, ignoring the fact that all the other guests were now looking at him. 'It's not safe.' And then, with a final twitch of his face, he was gone.

Ben blinked, then looked up at the youth hostel worker with a flicker of annoyance. He almost said something, but stopped himself at the last minute. 'Sorry about that,' he mumbled. 'He sort of latched onto me.'

'Mind if I sit down?' the receptionist asked. 'Name's Don, by the way.'

'Ben,' he replied shortly, shaking Don's hand.

'Was he bothering you, Ben?' Don asked.

Ben shrugged noncommittally: truth was, he didn't

really know the answer to that question. The old man still made him feel a bit jumpy, and the idea of him creeping around in this old stone building didn't make Ben feel particularly at ease; but he had found himself drawn in by what he'd been saying.

'He arrived here last night, a few hours after you. Says his name is Joseph. I put him in a dorm on his own – didn't think any of the other guests would really fancy sharing with him, and we're not busy.' Don stretched out, put his feet on the table and clasped his hands behind his head. 'We get quite a lot of them round here, to be honest.'

Ben didn't understand what he meant. 'A lot of what?'

Don looked around to check he wasn't being over-heard, then spoke in a softer voice. 'Nutters. Cranks. Spadeadam, you see. It attracts them. All the conspiracy theories – you wouldn't believe the stuff people make up about that place.' He rolled his eyes as if to indicate his disdain for such people.

'Right,' Ben replied, not wishing to let on that he was having his own doubts about the place.

'Anyway.' Don jumped up brightly. 'Part of my job is to look after any unaccompanied kids who stay here. Don't want you getting into any kind of trouble, do we? Let me know if he gives you any gyp.' With that he walked off.

Ben sat there in silence for a few minutes, deep in reflection and chewing on his fingernails. Conspiracy theories, he thought to himself. Don had laughed it off so easily, and under different circumstances no doubt Ben would have done too. But he couldn't get the image out of his head of the soldier shooting the two hen harriers earlier in the day. Whatever anybody said, *that* was a strange thing to happen, and the old man seemed quite sure he knew what was going on. He decided to try and find him, now, and ask him what he had been about to say when they had been interrupted. No doubt it would be nonsense, the ravings of a crazy mind; but at least Ben would be able to satisfy himself of that.

All the dormitories were on the first floor of the building, up a central flight of stone steps that clattered as he hurried up them. Turning right at the top of the steps led you to the dormitories that were in use – boys on the right, girls on the left – but Don had told Ben that the old man had been put somewhere else. Following little more than his instinct, Ben turned left.

In this direction, the corridor was less well lit – a single low-wattage bulb hanging from the ceiling was all the illumination it had. There were several doors on either side: tentatively, Ben tried them, but they were locked. Eventually, though, at the end of the corridor on the left, he found one that wasn't. He gently opened it. 'Hello,' he breathed into the darkness.

There was no reply, so he opened the door a little wider and stepped inside.

His hand fumbled for a moment for a light switch, but he couldn't find one. Instead he stood still and waited for his night vision to become accustomed to the darkness. It took a minute or two until he could see that he was indeed in a dormitory, but the beds were all empty. There was a general aroma of disuse about the place, and the large windows had no blinds or curtains: clearly this was not somewhere that was frequently used. Certainly there was no sign of the old man.

All of a sudden, Ben heard Don's overly cheery voice. For some reason he didn't want to be caught snooping around, so he closed the door behind him and stepped further into the room, crossing the wooden floorboards to the window. He looked out into the blackness.

Clouds were scudding past the almost-full moon, which was bright when it was in view. Mesmerized by their swift movement, Ben thought of the moonlit African nights he had seen in the Congo, and of the silent airborne majesty of the hen harriers earlier today. And then he thought of something Annie had said back in Macclesfield. 'We humans can do some pretty dumb things sometimes.'

Too right, Ben thought to himself. Like standing around in dark rooms looking for weird old men.

He was just about to turn and leave, however, when

he heard a noise from outside. Looking through the window, he saw, in the half-light of the moon, a figure. He was unmistakable really, in his grey overcoat. Ben watched as the old man walked as hurriedly as his frail legs could manage away from the house and faded into the impenetrable gloom.

And as he disappeared into the night, Ben felt as if the room in which he stood had suddenly grown colder.

He shook his head and turned round. The old man had spooked him at the train station – that much was obvious. It all seemed too much of a coincidence, him turning up here the next night, full of warnings and veiled threats; but that's what it was. A coincidence. Nothing more.

But in a corner of his mind, a nagging feeling would not go away. No matter how much he tried to twist things, to rationalize them, to make sense of them, one fact seemed to Ben to be perfectly clear.

The old man might be crazy, but whatever anyone said, something strange was going on at Spadeadam.

Chapter Five

Ben was tired, but could not sleep.

Everything seemed to be buzzing around in his head as he lay in the darkened dormitory, listening to the heavy breathing of the other hostel guests sleeping around him. The rain had started again, and he thought of the old man out there protected from the elements only by his dark grey overcoat. No doubt Don would dismiss his midnight wanderings as the crazy actions of someone who had lost his marbles, but suspicions still gnawed away at Ben, suspicions he couldn't quite put his finger on, but which troubled him nonetheless. He found himself repeating the conversation he had had with the old man time and again, trying to squeeze meaning out of it that he might have missed.

'Strange things happening at Spadeadam,' he had

said in his odd accent. 'Always have been, ever since I can remember, ever since Blue Streak.'

What did he mean? What was Blue Streak? Ben felt like he was trying to put a jigsaw together without knowing where all the pieces were.

Suddenly he remembered his PDA. Quietly, so as not to disturb any of his room-mates, he crept out of bed and rummaged among his things until he found it. Then, covering himself with his sleeping bag so that the glow from the screen did not wake anyone up, he switched it on. In seconds he had an Internet connection. He googled 'Blue Streak' and waited for the results.

What he discovered kept him reading for some time.

Blue Streak, he learned, was a rainbow code – one of a series of code names used in the middle of the last century to disguise the true nature of various British military research operations: code names like Black Arrow, a vehicle used to launch satellites, or Green Satin, an airborne navigation unit – but Blue Streak was more destructive than either of those. It was the secret name given to the development of a medium-range ballistic missile. After the Second World War, Britain had needed a nuclear deterrent in order to remain a world power. Blue Streak was to be it.

Ben blinked when he read where the central location of the Blue Streak project was. Spadeadam, just a couple of miles from where he lay at that very moment.

The Spadeadam test site was absolutely enormous. Before Blue Streak it was practically uninhabited, but soon large numbers of workers were brought in and a huge amount of construction work started: control bunkers, reservoirs, miles and miles of piping, engineering workshops and, most importantly, huge, concrete static test-beds. These giant structures were intended to test the missile engines which, when they were started, could be heard for miles around. Millions of gallons of water from a nearby river were pumped into the test-beds in order to cool the engines: as a result, enormous clouds of steam caused micro-climates far and wide over Spadeadam.

Blue Streak was always controversial, however, and MPs finally refused to allow the underground missile silos to be constructed because they were too expensive. In 1959, the Americans unveiled Skybolt, an aircraft-based missile, which made Blue Streak effectively redundant. The programme was never completed.

The end of Blue Streak did not mean that people stopped being interested in it, however; and for years, rumours circulated that there was more going on at Spadeadam than the government admitted to, or perhaps even knew about. Ben scoffed slightly when he read reports of mysterious personnel dressed in what looked like white spacesuits in remote parts of the base.

More believable was the rumour that had apparently gone round the local villages that Spadeadam housed an enormous underground hospital. Whatever the truth, it was clear to him that many people believed there were more secret, sinister things going on there.

Of course, he knew that already. He had just met one of them.

In 2004, the conspiracy theorists were given ammunition to back up their claims. An area of trees in the Spadeadam site needed to be cleared. It was a routine procedure, but what was discovered was very far from being routine: there were found to be extensive excavations for an underground missile silo, of exactly the type that was never supposed to have been built in Spadeadam. Investigations showed that no official plans of this silo existed, nor any other records whatsoever.

Clearly it had been a very official secret. Something the authorities did not want the man in the street to know about.

What was it the old man had said? 'Stay away from Spadeadam. It's not safe.'

Ben furrowed his forehead. Everything he was reading about had happened so long ago, during the Cold War – surely nobody believed in this day and age that suspicious things were still happening there. Did they? He decided to research Spadeadam a bit further.

In 1976, the RAF took over the Spadeadam site, and the following year they converted it into the world's first Electronic Warfare Tactics Range. Electronic warfare – Ben didn't really know what that meant, although he felt pretty sure Annie would be able to fill him in. But everywhere he looked, he found insinuations of cover-ups and secret operations going on within the boundaries of the Spadeadam site. Nothing concrete. Nothing official. Just rumours.

Ben wasn't sure if he thought it all made sense, or if he was even more confused than before. He switched off his PDA and lay there in the darkness, trying to piece together everything he had just read. There didn't seem to be much doubt about the fact that secret, classified government projects had been undertaken there in the past – the discovery of the hidden missile silo made that pretty clear. But all that was a long time ago. Cover-ups? Conspiracies? Surely that sort of thing didn't go on now. Did it?

With those thoughts spinning round in his brain, sleep gradually overcame Ben. It was a turbulent sleep, broken and full of ominous visions of missiles and concrete bunkers, of faceless gunmen and slaughtered birds, and above all the troubled, piercing green eyes of the old man whose words Ben could not seem to get out of his head.

'Strange things happening at Spadeadam . . .' His

voice seemed to echo in the darkness. 'Strange things happening at Spadeadam . . .'

Strange things indeed.

Ben awoke with a start.

He felt no sleepiness, just a sudden clarity. His dreams had been a jumble, but now something made perfect sense to him. When he had told the old man about the hen harrier, it had not seemed to surprise him at all. 'Makes perfect sense,' he had told Ben.

And suddenly, it did.

It was still dark outside – a glance at his watch told him that it was just past four o'clock – and Ben's first thought was for the old man. Was he still out there in the unwelcoming night, or had he crept back to the hostel before it had closed for the night to try and take advantage of its warmth and shelter? Somehow, he felt he knew the answer. He crept out of bed, sneaked illicitly into Annie's dormitory, and woke her up.

For a minute she didn't seem to know where she was, but she soon regained her bearings. 'What time is it?' she whispered hoarsely to Ben.

'Four o'clock, but you have to get up. I need to talk to you about something.'

'At four o'clock in the morning?'

'Yeah. Get your stuff ready – I'll meet you downstairs.'

The reception area was empty as Ben waited for her; finally she came down the stone steps carrying her rucksack, her face a thundercloud. Ben spoke before she could say a thing. 'We've got to go to Spadeadam.'

She looked at him like he was mad. 'What are you talking about, Ben?'

So Ben told her about the old man and how he had seen him wandering off into the night. 'We met in the common room last night and he kept talking about Spadeadam and Blue Streak. It's a—'

'I know what Blue Streak is, Ben. Don't tell me you've started to buy all those stupid conspiracy theories.'

'Listen,' Ben urged. 'It all makes sense. If you're doing something you want to keep secret, the last thing you want is random people walking around where they can stumble upon it, right?'

'I suppose so,' Annie replied reluctantly.

'Why have we come to the area?' Ben pressed.

'For the bird-watching.'

'Do you think they get many bird-watchers here?'

'Yeah, quite a few, I suppose.'

'Exactly. So what's the best way to stop bird-watchers coming to Spadeadam?'

The two cousins looked at each other, their faces serious.

'Are you trying to tell me,' Annie asked slowly, 'that

someone is shooting rare birds around here to stop bird-watchers trespassing into Spadeadam and discovering their . . . their . . . *secret plans*? Ben, Spadeadam is a serious place, an important facility. They train our soldiers well so that they don't lose their lives . . .'

When she put it like that, Ben realized how far-fetched it sounded; but the pieces of the jigsaw still fitted, and somehow he knew he was right. 'Can you think of another explanation?' he asked.

Annie was shaking her head. 'Nobody would do something as sick as that,' she told him.

Instantly, Ben thought back to the Democratic Republic of the Congo. 'Believe me,' he murmured, 'I've seen them do worse. Anyway' – he decided to try a different tack – 'what about the old man? He's not all there. I bet you any money you like he's gone to Spadeadam. I bet he's just wandering around there, getting freezing cold. We've got to try and find him, make sure he's all right.'

'Ben,' Annie told him patiently. 'You can't just go wandering into RAF Spadeadam. Do you have any idea what they do there?'

'Yeah.' Ben shrugged, trying to sound as if he knew what he was talking about. 'It's an electronic warfare tactics range.'

'And do you know what that means?'

'Er . . . no,' he admitted. 'Not really.'

Annie sighed. 'Electronic warfare,' she explained, her voice taking on an almost school-teacherly tone, 'or EW, is manipulating the electromagnetic spectrum to defeat or evade the enemy.'

'Right,' Ben replied. 'And in English?'

'Jamming radars, stealth technology, scrambling your enemy's signals and using your own electronic weapons to destroy them. My dad says it's the future of warfare. At Spadeadam, they simulate the effects of electronic warfare so that pilots can learn how to deal with it. They have dummy targets for aircraft to practise on under EW conditions.'

She must have realized that Ben was still looking at her a bit blankly, because when she spoke again it was much more slowly and clearly. 'Planes fly over Spadeadam and blow things up, Ben,' she stated. '*A lot.* And the army's EW research, a lot of which goes on at Spadeadam, really *is* top secret.'

Ben fell silent. He knew Annie had a fair point – trespassing on an RAF base was a dangerous business – but he just couldn't shake off his conviction that something untoward was happening there. He thought back to his experiences in Australia – all had not been as it seemed at the US base there. Maybe that was why he was not so convinced as Annie that everything was as it should be in Spadeadam. 'You're right,' he said quietly. 'We're going to have to be careful.'

'We're *not* going to have to be careful, Ben, because we're not going.'

Ben shrugged. 'Speak for yourself,' he said. He picked up the rucksack that was on the floor beside him and made for the door.

'Wait!' Annie told him. Ben smiled slightly to himself. He knew, despite her arguments, that Annie would not be able to resist a bit of intrigue. He turned to look at her. 'My dad's an air commodore,' she appealed to him. 'Can you imagine the trouble I'll be in if we're caught?'

'Then we'd better make sure we don't get caught, hadn't we?'

Annie's face was still filled with doubt. Ben had one last suggestion to try.

'Tell you what,' he said. 'I've got my digital camera here. We'll sneak into Spadeadam and see if we can find anyone shooting birds. If we do, I'll take a picture of them and we can show it to someone who can put a stop to it. But if we don't find anything by sunset, we'll leave and I'll never mention it again.'

For a moment Annie didn't reply and Ben could see that she was grappling with her conscience. Then she took a deep, slow breath. 'Do you promise, Ben?'

Ben nodded his head firmly. 'I promise.'

She closed her eyes. 'All right,' she said. 'When do we leave?'

Ben glanced back towards the exit.

'No time like the present,' he observed, as he opened the door and stepped out into the early morning.

Chapter Six

Pyongyang, North Korea

It was the rainy season in North Korea, and the season was living up to its name. Torrential rain fell through the humid air, so heavy that it blurred the bright red light of the twenty-five-metre-high torch on the top of the imposing Juche Tower. Lee Chin-Hwa gazed out at the hazy sight from the back of his Mercedes limousine – a luxury given only to party bureaucrats or those favoured by the regime. Few ordinary North Koreans had cars. If they wanted to see the splendour of the Juche Tower – built to commemorate the seventieth birthday of Kim Il Sung, the former Communist leader and father of the current leader, Kim Jong Il – they would have to walk. But nobody would be walking there at the moment. Not in this rain, and not at this time of the morning.

It was five o'clock and still dark. Lee Chin-Hwa had been awoken by a telephone call as he slept in the small apartment that he shared with his elderly mother on the outskirts of Pyongyang.

'Lee Chin-Hwa?' the harsh voice at the other end of the phone had asked.

'That's right,' he had replied groggily.

'There is a car waiting for you outside. You are required to attend the government offices.' There was a click as the phone was put down.

Chin-Hwa had always been interested in physics, ever since his schooldays when he had trudged dutifully every morning to the faceless concrete school near his parents' apartment block. His teachers, however, had been more interested in indoctrinating their pupils according to the regime's instructions. So instead of learning about atoms at school, he had learned about revolutionary history. And instead of learning about space, he had learned about the blessed life of Kim Il Sung. Only at home could he study the science that so excited him.

Chin-Hwa's father Ki-Woon had fought in the Korean War, during which time he had come into contact with some American soldiers. Through them he had learned a phrase which amused him, and which he used to repeat in his comic-sounding American accent every time he found Chin-Hwa reading one of his prized and illegal scientific textbooks: 'You can't keep a good man down!'

Ki-Woon had been a talented physicist himself. When Chin-Hwa was fifteen years old, however, his father had been instructed by the government to join those scientists involved in developing North Korea's nuclear programme. But Ki-Woon was a principled man: he was of the firm belief that science should be used for the good of mankind, not for its destruction.

He knew what he was doing. And he knew what the outcome would be.

It was just before midnight when the knock on the door came. Chin-Hwa shared a bedroom with his parents. He saw his father sit up promptly and exchange a meaningful glance with his mother, whose face was fixed in a mask of undisguised terror. He hugged her tightly, only untwining his arms when there was another, slightly louder knock. Then he climbed out of bed, pulled on his threadbare clothes, and hugged his son. 'It is up to you to look after your mother now,' he whispered in his ear.

Chin-Hwa and his mother followed timidly as Ki-Woon walked out into the main room of the apartment and opened the door.

Standing in the dimly lit corridor were three men. They were not wearing military uniform, but something about their demeanour made it clear that they were here on official business. One of them – clearly the leader of their little gang – spoke. 'Lee Ki-Woon?'

Chin-Hwa's father nodded.

'You have to come with us.'

'On what business?'

The man smiled nastily. 'On the business of His Excellency the President, on suspicion of treason.'

A sob escaped the lips of Chin-Hwa's mother as, head held high, her husband started walking through the doorway.

'Wait!' the man said, holding up the palm of his hand. 'Your son too. He must come.'

A horrible silence descended, and Chin-Hwa felt a chill run through his body. And then he heard it: the scream of his mother. 'Not my son! Please, not my son! He has nothing to do with this. He is innocent.'

The men at the door looked suddenly panicked. 'Shut her up,' their leader told Ki-Woon harshly. 'Shut the woman up now!'

Ki-Woon glanced back at his family. 'There is nothing I can do,' he said. 'If you take her son away from her, she will scream like that until the end of her days.' He raised an eyebrow at the group as his wife's wails continued. 'Of course, if she carries on screaming just for the next few minutes, she will attract attention.

People will come to see what is the matter, and you three will be revealed for the government informers that you are. Things will go badly for you then, I think.'

The men looked nervously at each other.

'I will come with you,' Ki-Woon continued quietly. 'But if you insist on bringing my son, I swear I will fight you with every bone in my body. You will have to kill me here and now, in front of all the neighbours who will surely be at our door very soon.'

The man stared at Ki-Woon; Ki-Woon returned his gaze without letting the fear that he must surely have been feeling show on his face.

'Grab him,' the man said finally, and his two accomplices stepped inside the flat and each took an arm.

Ki-Woon did not struggle. He just turned his head round to look at his son. 'Remember what I told you, Chin-Hwa,' he said.

Seconds later, he was gone. Chin-Hwa never saw him again.

That was seventeen years ago. Barely a day passed when Chin-Hwa did not wonder what had happened to his father. He knew he would never find out, although he could make a pretty good guess. In the north of the country were the notorious prison camps where hundreds of thousands of political dissidents were sent. Torture was commonplace in such places. The lucky ones died soon after they arrived.

Ki-Woon's son had obeyed his father's instructions, taking care of his mother as she slipped into an old age full of sorrow. His interest in science had not abated, but he had made a conscious decision to avoid studying nuclear physics. The government's passion for becoming a nuclear power was well known, and he had no desire to be forced into helping them. When the regime was finally overthrown – as surely it must be someday soon – he wanted his skills to be of use, and so he had studied electronics and computing in his spare time, while making a living fixing the antiquated wiring systems of the cheaply built apartment blocks around the capital.

Every couple of months he had saved up enough to spend an hour on the heavily filtered workstations at Pyongyang's only Internet cafés – no doubt the authorities had known that he was looking at sites informing him of the latest advances in the world of electronics. But they left him alone – theirs was a Cold-War mentality and they were interested only in bombs.

A year ago, however, it had all changed.

He had arrived home at lunch time to find his mother sitting frightened in the one armchair they possessed. A man he did not recognize, smartly dressed in a khaki military suit with shiny shoes, stood nearby.

'Who are you?' Chin-Hwa demanded of him.

'Lee Chin-Hwa?' the man asked, ignoring the question.

'That's right.'

'Ah, good. I was just telling your mother that I have brought you a gift.' He handed him a small white envelope. Chin-Hwa's eyes narrowed and he looked inside. Banknotes. At a guess, Chin-Hwa would have said there were 3,000 won there – more than he earned in a month. 'Come with me,' the man instructed. 'I would like to show you something.'

Chin-Hwa knew he couldn't refuse.

The official – Chin-Hwa would never find out his name – escorted him to a waiting chauffeured Mercedes. In silence they drove to an area on the out-skirts of the city where there was a large athletics field. A crowd had gathered, but there were no sportsmen. Sickened, Chin-Hwa knew what they were here to witness.

'Get out,' the official told him.

Together they joined the waiting crowd.

After a couple of minutes, a white minibus drove up. It stopped in front of the crowd and four armed soldiers jumped out. They opened up the back and bundled out five people, their eyes blindfolded and their hands tied behind their back. The people were lined up. One of them fell to his knees through fear, and was roughly pulled to his feet, then three of the armed soldiers formed a line a few metres from them. The fourth soldier started to shout commands.

'Ready your weapons!'

'Aim at the enemy!'

'Fire!'

The rifles cracked and the prisoners fell as one to the ground; Chin-Hwa, nauseated, averted his eyes.

'Fire!'

A second shot, just to be sure.

'Cease firing!'

The soldier turned to the crowd. 'You have witnessed,' he shouted, 'how these miserable fools have ended up. Traitors who betray the nation and its people end up like this.'

The official turned to Chin-Hwa. 'Miserable fools,' he whispered, echoing the soldier's words. 'They knew what would happen to them.'

Chin-Hwa didn't reply. He was too busy trying not to be sick.

'Your mother is frail,' the official continued. 'It would be a pity if she were to end up like those miserable fools, would it not?'

Chin-Hwa froze for a moment. He turned to the official. 'What do you mean?'

The official just raised an eyebrow and gave a know-ing look towards the dead bodies only a few metres away from them. 'Of course,' he said, 'it's up to you. If you make the right decision, she could enjoy a long and happy old age. You'll even get one of those white envelopes every month to make her more comfortable.'

Chin-Hwa closed his eyes and took a deep breath. 'All right,' he said. 'You win. What is it that you want from me?'

The official smiled. 'Well,' he said, ushering Chin-Hwa back to the waiting car, 'that is rather complicated.'

And so it had all started

Every week since then, and sometimes twice a week, the reluctant scientist had been escorted by the same black limousine in which he now sat on that rainy morning, to the government building of the Supreme People's Assembly. What he had learned there he never told anyone, even his mother. It was not just because he had been forbidden to do so; it was because he was ashamed. Ashamed of being a part of what was going on. Ashamed that, unlike his father before him, he was unable to refuse to use his scientific knowledge for purposes such as this.

As the limousine drove him closer to the government buildings, Chin-Hwa remembered that day seventeen years ago when his father had been taken from them. Ki-Woon had told him to look after his mother. Well, in a way that was what he was doing. He wondered if his father would have accepted that as an excuse for being involved in the government's terrible plans. He wondered what his father would have done.

A few months previously, there had been a buzz on the streets of North Korea. The government had announced that it was to dismantle its nuclear reactor. It had been hinting to the world that its nuclear capabilities would soon be given up. This was cause for optimism, everybody said. A turning point. There was hope for a new future.

But they didn't know what Chin-Hwa knew.

They hadn't heard the powerful men talking.

They hadn't seen the plans.

They didn't know about Vortex.

Chapter Seven

The early-morning mist hovered eerily above the marshland.

Ben and Annie stood silently at a barbed-wire boundary fence to RAF Spadeadam, only a hundred metres away from where they had witnessed the shooting of the hen harrier the previous day. In front of them was a metal sign on a post. It seemed out of place here, in the middle of this vast expanse of nature where there were no roads or electricity pylons or any of the usual debris of modern life. Its message was clear enough, however: DANGER. LOW-FLYING AIRCRAFT. LIVE AMMUNITION TRAINING. KEEP OUT.

Ben Tracey stared at it, hotly aware of the prickly silence emanating from his cousin. 'How are we going to get in?' he asked, half to himself. The fence was not that high – perhaps only as high as Ben himself – but it was covered by a wicked-looking roll of barbed wire that meant they could never climb over it without ripping their skin to shreds; and the fence itself was constructed of lines of barbed wire close together which meant they couldn't squeeze through.

He glanced at Annie. She had barely said a word since they'd left the youth hostel – her way, Ben realized, of making her thoughts about their expedition entirely clear – but he noticed that she was looking up and down the fence with interest, clearly trying to work out a way in. He smiled to himself. Annie wasn't the sort of person to let something like a bit of barbed wire get in her way.

As she stared at the fence, Ben had an idea. He put his hand in his pocket and pulled out a Swiss Army penknife that had lingered unused in his bedroom for a couple of years, but which he had picked up on a whim as he left home. From the many blades, he selected a small pair of pliers, then approached the barbed wire and attempted to cut through them. It only took one snip, however, to realize that the pliers were far too flimsy for the job: they buckled and dented as Ben cursed and struggled to fold them away back into the penknife before returning it to his pocket.

His eyes flicked to Annies rucksack. 'I suppose you bird-watchers don't have much call for a good pair of wire-cutters,' he said archly.

Annie ignored the question and continued scanning up and down the fence. Finally she spoke.

'The posts.'

Ben raised an eyebrow at her. 'What?'

'The posts,' Annie repeated. 'They're made of wood, I think.' She trotted towards one of the posts that held the fence up at regular intervals, and rapped her hand against it. 'Wood,' she confirmed with a certain sense of satisfaction.

'Great,' Ben said, coming up to join her. 'So what?'

'It looks pretty old and weathered, that's all,' Annie replied. 'A few good kicks and we might be able to knock it down.'

'Do you think?'

Annie shrugged. 'It's not really seriously designed to keep people out, is it? I mean, like you said, if you really want to get in, all you have to do is bring a pair of wire-cutters, or some pliers or something. It's just a deterrent, a safety measure – like that sign.' She eyed it up again. 'A few good kicks near the top of the post should do it.'

Annie removed her rucksack from her back and handed it to him. She looked down at her heavy, muddy walking boots and furrowed her forehead. 'Not the ideal shoes,' she muttered, taking a couple of steps back then looking towards the post and sizing it up. She raised her arms and appeared to balance herself.

The first kick took Ben by surprise. Annie jumped up and struck the post near the top, before landing cat-like back on her feet again. The post wobbled slightly, sending shockwaves repeating down the wire fence on either side. 'It'll come,' Annie said with satisfaction.

It took four kicks before the bottom of the post started to split. When that happened, Ben put Annie's rucksack on the ground, dropped his own, and assisted by using his strength to push the post down onto its side. The fence dipped with it. 'We should be able to walk along the post and jump over the top of the barbed wire,' Ben observed as he picked up his rucksack. He turned to Annie and grinned. 'Nice one,' he said. 'You really are my partner in crime now.'

'Yeah.' Annie rolled her eyes at him. 'Well, if we get caught, I'm telling them it was all your stupid idea.' Deftly she skipped onto the post and jumped over the boundary. A few seconds later, they were both in.

They had only gone from one side of the fence to another – hardly any distance at all – but somehow it felt different on the other side. More exposed. Ben had the impression Annie felt it too. As soon as they had made it across the fence, they both started looking around a bit shiftily, trying to see if anyone was watching them. Ben found he was glad of the mist.

'Where to now, pathfinder?' Annie asked in a hushed voice.

Ben thought for a moment. 'Well,' he said, 'there's no point following the boundary now that we've crossed over. And anyway, however he managed to get in, I'm sure the old man will have headed towards the centre of Spadeadam rather than skirting around the edges.' He pointed in a direction that was at right angles to the fence. 'So I guess it means that way.'

Annie inclined her head. 'Whatever you say,' she agreed, and strode out in the direction Ben had indicated.

As they walked, the ground became marshy underfoot and the mist, which had been hovering around their knees, became thicker and more pervasive. It wasn't long before they were unable to see more than twenty metres in any direction. 'It's getting cold,' Annie said after a while.

Ben nodded. 'Hopefully the sun will burn this mist off as it gets later. Maybe we should stop and put an extra jumper on.'

'Good idea,' Annie replied, shivering. She peered through the mist. 'Is that a copse of trees up ahead?'

Ben looked. Sure enough he could see the ghostly outline of some trees a little way in front of them. 'Let's get there,' he said. 'We can put on some warm clothes and have a look at the map. Maybe the trees will be marked, and it'd be a good idea to keep track of where we are.'

It didn't take them long to reach the trees. Ben and Annie dumped their rucksacks with a certain amount of relief – walking through the marshy terrain was a lot harder work than they'd expected, and they were glad of a few moments' rest. Once they had rummaged around and found a jumper each, they sat on top of their rucksacks and ate some chocolate to give them a bit of instant energy and warmth.

'I can't believe it isn't even autumn yet,' Ben commented. 'I suppose they won't be doing much in the way of live ammo training today.'

'Why not?'

'Well,' Ben faltered, 'the mist, I suppose. Difficult for planes to see and everything.'

'Oh, come on, Ben,' Annie replied with a smile. 'It's not the First World War, you know. Pilots don't fly by sight alone. Anyway' – she looked around her and then upwards – 'this mist might seem thick to us, but it's probably just ground cover. Like you say, it'll burn away—'

'Shhhhh!' Ben interrupted her, holding up his hand and straining his ear to hear.

Annie fell silent. 'What is it?' she mouthed.

They both sat perfectly still. There was a shuffling sound nearby, but for some reason the mist seemed to obscure where it was coming from.

It stopped, and all around them seemed deadly

quiet. Ben and Annie looked at each other, neither of them able to stop an expression of worry from showing in their faces. In his mind's eye, Ben saw the image of the soldier from yesterday, the one who had shot down the birds, and he found himself holding his breath, acutely aware of the heavy thump-thump of his own heartbeat.

The shuffling started up again. This time there was no mistaking the regular pattern of footsteps.

Somebody coughed, a harsh, hacking, sandpaper sound that echoed through the still, early-morning air. And then the footsteps. Regular. Determined. And coming nearer.

It was only by chance that Ben was looking in the right direction to see the figure approaching out of the mist. It was just a shadow at first, a silhouette becoming gradually more distinct as it approached. Ben lightly brushed Annie's hand to get her attention, then pointed in the direction of the figure. They watched, wide-eyed, as it approached.

He was muttering to himself, the old man. His head was bowed, but although he walked slowly he was not as infirm as some people his age might have been. As he came closer, Ben could hear him muttering, a low, indistinct murmur of words that made no sense to his ears. Occasionally he would stop, raise his head and look all around. He seemed for all the world as though he were searching for something, but each time he did it, Ben had the impression that he believed himself to be somewhere completely different to where he was ten seconds ago. He strained his ears, desperately trying to catch some of that indecipherable muttering, but it was impossible. Ben couldn't help thinking that there *were* no real words coming out of the old man's mouth.

Just as Ben thought he was going to walk straight towards them, he stopped, looked around once more, and veered off in a different direction. But when he came to the trees, he halted and sat down against one of them, just as Ben and Annie had done.

The two of them sat in silence for a moment. 'He didn't see us,' Annie breathed. Ben looked at her and saw anxiety etched on her face – the arrival of the old man had clearly frightened her a bit, and if Ben was honest he would have to admit to feeling a bit spooked himself.

The old man was rummaging inside a plastic carrier bag now. He pulled out a Thermos flask and, with slightly shaky hands, unscrewed it and poured himself a cup of something hot. He breathed in the welcome steam escaping from his cup and closed his eyes, as though that simple thing had given him more pleasure than anyone could know, then he sipped gratefully before resting his head against the bark of the tree.

'I feel a bit sorry for him,' Annie whispered.

'Yeah, me too. See why I wanted to come and find him? Look, I'm going to go and talk to him—'

'No, don't,' Annie said, just a bit too quickly.

'He's harmless, Annie,' Ben assured her.

Annie responded with a wide-eyed, uncharacteristically frightened look.

'Come on,' Ben said reassuringly. 'I'll show you.' He stood up, and started walking towards the old man, with Annie close behind.

'Joseph!' he called gently when he was near enough for the old man to see them, but not so close that he would be too alarmed by their presence. 'It is Joseph, isn't it?'

The old man looked up like a startled animal, spilling his hot tea over his hand as he did so. The scalding liquid didn't seem to worry him.

'How do you know my name?' Joseph hissed. 'Who are you?'

'I'm Ben,' Ben replied confidently and with a smile. 'We spoke last night in the youth hostel. Do you remember?'

Joseph seemed to shrink back against the tree, looking first at Ben then at Annie. There was not even a spark of recognition in his face.

'We talked about this place,' Ben persisted. 'About Spadeadam. You told me about Blue Streak. Don't you remember?'

The old man started nodding his head furiously. 'Blue Streak, yes,' he gabbled. 'Spadeadam. Strange things happening at Spadeadam. *Strange things.*'

His voice crumbled once more into a meaningless mutter and Ben and Annie cast an anxious look at each other. 'I thought you said he'd recognize you,' Annie breathed.

Ben grimaced, then looked back at the old man before taking a tentative step forward. As he did so, his foot landed on a twig. It cracked, the noise sounding much louder than it should do. Instantly the old man stood up, his hawk-like eyes peering at Ben. He held the now empty cup above his shoulder as if it were a missile that he was prepared to hurl. 'Stay away,' he warned. 'Who are you? Why are you following me?'

'We just want to make sure you're OK,' Ben said in what he hoped was a reassuring tone of voice.

Again the old man peered at Ben and Annie, as though looking at them for the first time. 'Kids,' he said shortly. 'Spadeadam's not a place for kids. You must leave, now. Leave me alone. Get out of here.'

'But, Joseph—'

'*Get out!*' the old man roared, and for a moment Ben thought he saw real madness in his eyes. Both he and Annie stepped nervously back.

The old man looked around him yet again, and started muttering once more. This time, Ben managed to catch something of what Joseph was saying. 'I have to find the place,' he was whispering to himself. 'They don't know I'm here, and I have to find the place.'

'What place, Joseph?' Ben called with a confidence he did not feel. 'Who doesn't know you're here?'

Joseph shook his head. 'Leave me alone. And get out of here. You *have* to get out of here.' He turned away from them, picked up his plastic bag and returned the Thermos flask, then walked further into the trees. The deeper he walked into the copse, the more in-distinct he became in the mist, but before he disappeared from sight, he turned round to speak to them once more. For an alarming moment, his bright green eyes seemed to shine like emeralds in the mist, clear and knowing. 'Leave me alone,' he called again, before continuing on his way.

Ben and Annie watched as the figure of the old man grew increasingly ghostly among the trees. Ben stepped forward after him. 'Come on,' he said suddenly. 'We have to try and talk to him again, find out what he's on about.'

But Annie had grabbed him by the arm. 'Ben, he's incredibly frightened, can't you see? Keep disturbing him and we'll send the poor guy over the edge.'

Ben looked anxiously after him. 'What are we going to do, then?'

Annie bit her lip. Ben half expected her to suggest that they go home, but when she spoke it became clear to him that she was as intrigued by Joseph and his mysterious warnings as he was.

'Let's follow him, from a distance. We'll have to be careful and keep out of sight, but at least we'll be able to see that he's OK.'

Ben nodded. They grabbed their rucksacks, put them on and then, as silently as they could manage, started to trek deeper into the forest. And deeper into RAF Spadeadam.

Chin-Hwa's driver had deposited him outside the government building a couple of hours ago. He had rushed inside in a matter of seconds, but the heavy rain had still saturated his cheap clothes. Since then, he had been waiting on his own in a bare, chilly room containing nothing but a few old plastic chairs. There was no point asking anybody how long it would be until he was seen: Chin-Hwa would be called when his presence was required, and no sooner.

The door opened and an expressionless government worker appeared. He spoke to Chin-Hwa in a voice devoid of respect. 'They will see you now,' he said.

Chin-Hwa nodded, and followed the government worker out of the room and along a succession of corridors that all seemed identical. In all the time he had been coming here, Chin-Hwa had never managed to learn his way around. Sometimes he wondered if the place had been built like that on purpose.

Finally the government worker stopped outside another door and knocked respectfully before opening it.

'The scientist,' he announced to whoever was waiting inside. He stepped aside and allowed Chin-Hwa to enter.

There were four people in the room, the same four Chin-Hwa met with every time he came here. They wore suits that marked them out as high-ranking government men, but Chin-Hwa had immediately recognized them from their pictures in the newspaper when they had first met. The most important of them – the man to whom they all seemed to defer – sat at the head of the table. Behind him was a large picture.

Everybody in North Korea recognized the man in that picture. Kim Il Sung – president until his death in 1994, when his son Kim Jong Il succeeded him as leader and declared his father Eternal President of the Republic. His picture hung at every train station and in every school; there were more than 800 statues of the Eternal President scattered around the country. Not knowing who he was would be unthinkable.

The leader of the government group nodded cursorily at Chin-Hwa. 'Sit down,' he instructed.

Chin-Hwa took his place at the table. 'The Vortex device will be delivered the day after tomorrow, as discussed,' the leader informed the assembled group.

The other three government officials nodded in satisfaction; Chin-Hwa did his best not to let dismay show in his face.

The leader turned to one of the officials. 'We are sure that the British government knows nothing of what is happening?'

The official nodded. 'The British scientists developing the device work in secret, and the military personnel at the RAF camp are ignorant of their activities, with the exception of a handful of renegade officers who have a serious financial incentive to keep the research private.'

'Good,' the leader replied. He turned to Chin-Hwa. 'And you,' he said abruptly. 'You are sure that once the weapon is in our hands, you will be able to examine it and copy its design?'

Chin-Hwa's lips went thin. He had never made such a claim, but he knew that to suggest he couldn't do this was to sign his own death warrant. 'I am sure,' he replied quietly.

'Good,' the leader replied. 'I can now inform you of the president's wishes. Before Vortex is delivered to us here, he wishes to establish that it will be operational. He has instructed that it be tested on a major Western city.'

89

Chin-Hwa's eyes narrowed. He looked around the room for any sign of concern on the faces of the assembled officials, but he saw none. It was hardly surprising, of course – they all knew the implications of questioning the president's wisdom. But in a moment of recklessness, Chin-Hwa felt he could not let the silence that followed go unbroken. He coughed. 'May I ask,' he said, his head bowed humbly, 'what the president's target is?'

The leader looked at him impassively, as though wondering whether or not to allow that piece of information to be relayed. Finally he spoke.

'London,' he said. 'And when we have established that it works, there will be strikes against New York, Los Angeles and Madrid.'

His words seemed to echo around the room as they sank in.

Chin-Hwa knew he should not speak, but he couldn't help it. 'And, respectfully, the president is aware of what Vortex can do? He is aware of its capabilities? Of the devastation it can cause? Of the lives that will be lost?'

There was a horrible silence. The leader blinked.

'You question the wisdom of his excellency the president?'

Chin-Hwa bowed his head again. 'No,' he muttered. 'No, of course not.'

The leader nodded. 'Good,' he said shortly. 'You may leave us now.'

Chin-Hwa scraped his chair back and stood up. He bowed awkwardly to the officials, then left the room, desperately wanting to be out of there as quickly as possible, but not daring to move with anything other than a measured, calm slowness.

The Korean officials watched in frosty silence as the bumbling scientist left the room. Even after he closed the door behind him they remained quiet for a moment.

'Was it wise to tell him of our plans?' the first official said finally.

'It was necessary,' the leader replied. 'When we make our first strike against London, people will hear of it. It is not a good idea that it should be a surprise to him.' He turned to a second official. 'Are you sure he can be trusted?' he asked.

'We have no reason to believe otherwise,' the official replied. 'He is being closely watched, and does not appear to have mentioned Vortex to anyone.' The official smiled coldly. 'He will do anything to keep his mother safe, it seems.'

'Be that as it may,' the leader responded, 'there is no room for error.' He turned to look at the picture on the wall. 'The Eternal President would never have approved of his son's unwise decision to weaken our military capabilities. It is essential that the Vortex device is delivered to us if we are to be successful in our coup against the government. I want the surveillance on the scientist doubled. If he so much as thinks about jeopardizing our plans, I want him arrested. He can do his work just as easily from a prison cell as a laboratory. Are my instructions clear?'

The three officials nodded. 'They are clear,' they said in unison.

Chapter Eight

As the morning wore on, the mist dispersed. In one way that was good — it meant that it was easier to trail Joseph at a safe distance. But in another way it made things more difficult. As he had done ever since they had seen him, Joseph kept stopping and looking around: each time he did this, they had to stop and take cover behind a tree. But he never saw them, and after a while they found that they could be a little less wary. Joseph didn't seem to know what was going on around him.

After about an hour of following him, they reached the other side of the woods. Joseph stepped out from under the canopy of the trees, his eyes blinking in the sudden bright sunshine. Ben and Annie edged quietly towards the boundary of the trees and, doing their best to remain hidden, peered out. The sky was blue now, with only a few cotton-wool clouds floating high above. But it was not the sky that was grabbing their attention; it was what was on the ground.

In front of them was a road. It was not a new road, and it didn't look as if it had been used for many years. Potholes covered the surface, and the top dressing was loose and gravel-strewn. Beyond the road was a collection of concrete huts. Some of them were crumbling, others weren't; a few looked as if they had been utterly destroyed. But those that were still standing all had marks of discolouration from years of exposure to rain and the elements. These were old huts, and they covered a large area.

And somewhere in the middle of the huts, there was a tank.

Joseph had stopped by the side of the road. He was standing still, just staring at what he had stumbled across. Ben and Annie watched in silence as he stepped forward, tripping slightly on one of the potholes in the road as he crossed but managing to stay upright. As he entered the little commune of huts, he brushed his hand against the concrete, all the while looking around him in a kind of wonder. He was too far away for them to hear, but Ben could see from the movement of his lips when he occasionally turned in their direction that he was still muttering to himself – perhaps a bit more furiously now.

When he came to the tank, he appeared not even to notice it. Instead he leaned against the green metal of the huge armoured vehicle, facing back towards the woods, his eyes darting around as he continued to look at all the concrete huts. Ben hid behind a huge tree trunk and took his binoculars out of his rucksack, then surreptitiously looked through them to watch Joseph. 'He seems a bit calmer now,' he told Annie, observing that the old man seemed to be breathing deeply in a way that suggested he was trying to take control of himself. He put the binoculars down. 'I wonder what that tank's doing there in the middle of nowhere.'

Annie took the binoculars and studied the vehicle. 'Chieftain Mark Ten,' she said. 'Combat weight fifty-five tons, crew four, maximum speed forty-eight kilometres an hour. Armed with a hundred-and-twenty-millimetre tank gun with laser range finder, rate of fire eight rounds per minute. These Chieftains were in use until the early nineties when they were replaced by the Challenger.' She sounded, Ben thought, like a walking encyclopaedia.

'Blimey, Annie,' he said. 'Is there anything about this sort of stuff that you *don't* know?'

Annie gave him a winsome little smile. 'Not really,' she replied, fluttering her eyelashes girlishly at him.

Ben smiled. 'So, this Chieftain Mark ten. What exactly is it doing in the middle of a bunch of falling-down huts?'

'Ah,' Annie said, clearly enjoying showing off her knowledge, 'I thought you might ask that. It's a target, I should think.'

'A target? What do you mean?'

Annie put the binoculars back up to her eyes and looked through them towards Joseph and the tank as she spoke. 'I told you, this place is designed as target practice for aircraft. They take machinery like that Chieftain that's gone out of service, decommission them, strip them down and let people take pot shots at them.'

'Why go to all that trouble?' Ben asked. 'I mean, if it's not a real tank, it might as well be anything, mightn't it?'

Annie lowered the binoculars. 'Not really,' she said. 'I reckon that's a moving target.'

Ben was puzzled. 'I thought you said it was decommissioned.'

'I did. What they do is, they install a guidance mechanism that allows the tank to be moved remotely. Then, when there's a training exercise, they can operate the tank from a point of safety.'

'A remote control tank?'

'Something like that.'

'Cool.' Ben grinned.

Annie rolled her eyes. 'It's a serious—' she started to say.

But she was interrupted.

In the background, seemingly from nowhere, they heard a noise. It was a low drone, quiet at first but rapidly becoming louder. Ben and Annie looked at each other; then they looked at Joseph, all alone by the tank, oblivious to the danger that was fast approaching.

'Is that what I think it is?' Ben asked.

Annie, her face suddenly very serious, nodded.

'We have to get him away from there!' Ben said, louder now to make himself heard over the noise. 'If anyone sees him—'

But before Annie could reply, a fighter jet zoomed overhead. It seemed to be flying incredibly low – not much higher than the trees in which they were hiding – and the roar of the engines was like a thunderclap, resounding through the sky like some booming, airborne drum. It seemed to make the ground shake and sent a shock of sound waves through Ben and Annie, who both instinctively threw their hands over their ears, Annie dropping the binoculars as she did so.

As quickly as the plane had arrived, it was gone; but the noise was still there, the approaching drone that told them there would be more where that had come from.

His hands still over his ears, Ben looked at Joseph. The old man's reaction had been quite different from theirs. He stood defiantly among the huts, shaking his fist up to the sky and shouting something that

Ben could not hear because of the approaching noise.

With a sense of sudden panic, Ben remembered the sign they had seen at the boundary fence: DANGER. LOW-FLYING AIRCRAFT. LIVE AMMUNITION TRAINING. KEEP OUT. He looked at Annie. 'It's just a fly-over, right? These things aren't going to have any live ammo?' he shouted.

The look Annie returned did not fill him with confidence, but he didn't have time to question her further, because at that moment another plane thundered over. It was slightly higher this time, and further to Ben's right.

Neither of them saw the bomb being dropped – it was too small and too fast for that – but they certainly saw the explosion. One of the concrete huts on the outskirts of the little village exploded noisily into a cloud of dust and debris. Joseph's head turned swiftly to see the devastation, and as though it had injected a sudden clarity into his mind, he started to run in the opposite direction.

He didn't get far, however. A third aircraft sped over to Ben's left, dropping another bomb. This one failed to hit a target, instead blowing a massive crater in the earth, the tremors of which threw the old man heavily to the ground.

'We've got to help him!' Ben shouted, but Annie was already running in Joseph's direction, oblivious to the danger overhead. Ben followed.

And as soon as they were out from under the safety of the trees, the sky seemed to be full of rocketing aircraft, and the air thick with weaponry. Four bombs exploded before Ben and Annie managed to reach Joseph; as each one hit the ground, the earth seemed to shake and it was all they could do to keep their balance. 'Call this a training exercise!' Ben yelled at Annie.

'Don't try and tell me I didn't warn you, Ben,' Annie screamed back. 'These guys don't practise bombing people with basketballs, you know.'

Joseph was still on the ground when they reached him, frozen in wide-eyed terror at the noise and the danger around him.

'Joseph!' Ben shouted. 'We've got to get out of here. Do you understand?'

Joseph stared back at him, not even a shred of recognition in his face.

'*Joseph!*' Ben repeated. 'We're in danger! Get to your feet!'

But all the old man could do was stare, ashen-faced and terrified, from Ben to the planes.

Ben turned to Annie. 'Come on,' he instructed. 'We've got to get him to his feet. Help me.'

Annie nodded purposefully, then stepped to one side of the old man and grabbed him under his arm. Ben took the other. Before they could heave him up, however, a nearby hut exploded. They all hit the ground and started choking as they breathed in the sudden cloud of dust that billowed around them. There was a brief moment of respite, of relative quiet, but it was soon replaced by the ominous crescendo of another fighter jet. Ben and Annie knew they couldn't stick around to let their eyes and their lungs clear. They had to get back to the safety of the trees, so they heaved Joseph to his feet and started urging him away. The area was fast resembling a war zone . . .

Ben's ears were numb now from the constant boom of the planes' engines overhead, his throat burning from the dust. There seemed to be no let-up as the target practice continued. The trees were about thirty metres away, on the other side of the dirt track. Stumbling, they edged closer.

Twenty-five metres.

Twenty metres.

Annie started to cough, the dust in her lungs clearly getting to her. She faltered and stumbled.

'We're nearly there!' Ben shouted. 'We can't stop now. One of those bombs could get us at any time.'

Annie's face screwed up into a grimace of pure concentration. She nodded forcefully, then carried on heaving Joseph towards the woods.

They would have made it if he hadn't started to struggle.

It wasn't clear to Ben what had got the old man so

agitated, but something had. As the aircraft continued to fly over, his arms started to flail and, taken by surprise by his sudden show of strength, Ben and Annie lost their grip on him. Joseph ran, but not towards the woods. Instead he seemed to be heading towards one of the huts, not far from the road. It seemed older than most, more weathered and stained but still whole.

'Joseph!' Ben screamed, holding his arms over his head as if that would be any protection from the flying chunks of debris. 'Not that way! We have to get to the trees! *To the trees, Joseph!*'

But if Joseph heard, he wasn't listening.

'He's going to get us all killed,' Annie shouted.

Ben knew she could be right. He looked sharply towards the woods – they were close enough for him and Annie to get there safely and quickly. Maybe they should just make a run for it: if Joseph wanted to stand in the middle of a live ammo exercise, that was his look-out. But then he looked back towards the old man. He was staring at the hut, oblivious to the chaos around him. He wasn't in any kind of position to help himself.

Ben took a deep breath. 'You go,' he told his cousin. 'Get to the woods. I'm going after Joseph.'

Annie stood for a moment, her gaze alternating between the woods, Ben and the old man. 'You can't manage him by yourself,' she said. 'I'm coming with you.'

Ben saw the determination on her face and didn't even bother to argue.

'But, Ben . . .' Annie added breathlessly.

'What?'

'As soon as we've got him to safety, we're getting out of Spadeadam, OK?'

'Too right,' Ben agreed fervently.

Together they sprinted towards the old man.

They started running just as another plane screamed overhead, unloading its ammunition onto a rough patch of ground nearby. As the bomb fell, so did Annie. She screamed as she hit the ground. 'You all right?' Ben bellowed.

'Yeah,' she replied through gritted teeth, allowing Ben to pull her back up to her feet; but he noticed that as they continued to run towards Joseph she was limping a little.

By the time they got to the hut, Joseph was standing in front of the door. Even amid the panic, Ben could see an enigmatic smile on the old man's face as he stepped forward and opened the rickety metal door.

'We can't go inside the hut, Joseph.' Ben was so out of breath that it almost hurt to speak. 'The planes are aiming for them – it's too dangerous. You've got to come with us – it'll be safer in the trees, they're not a target.'

He stepped forward to seize the old man's arm, but

Joseph brushed him off with unexpected vigour, opened the door and stepped inside.

Ben looked at Annie, who glanced over her shoulder longingly at the safety of the trees. 'We can't . . .' she started to say, but her voice trailed off. They both realized that if they wanted to help Joseph, they would have to get him out of that hut, at least while the training exercise was going on.

'Ready?' he asked.

Annie closed her eyes. 'This was meant to be a quiet weekend bird-watching,' she muttered to herself before looking directly at her cousin. 'Ready,' she responded.

They stepped inside.

It was dark in the hut, but the open door gave them enough light to be able to see inside. It gave the impression of being a disused office, with a rickety old tin table against one wall, and a rusting filing cabinet against the other. As another plane flew overhead, Ben found himself wondering how long it had been since anyone had used this place. Many years, he decided. 'Come on, Joseph,' he heard Annie saying urgently. 'We've *got* to get out of here.'

Joseph was standing in the middle of the room, looking around him with a sense of wonder, as though he were taking in the glories of some royal palace. 'This is it,' he whispered to himself. 'This is it.'

Quickly, he stepped towards the filing cabinet, and

before Ben or Annie could say or do anything, he pushed it sharply. The empty cabinet clattered noisily onto one side.

The ringing metal seemed to echo against the concrete walls of the hut. And as the sound settled down, Ben found himself aware of something else.

It was silent outside.

He heard Annie breathe out heavily with relief. 'Thank heavens for that,' she said. 'It sounds like they've finished.'

But Ben didn't reply, because now there was something else to attract his attention – the same thing that Joseph was staring at, his face serious and any glimmer of madness in his eyes now gone. He took his cousin gently by the arm and pointed at the area of floor where the filing cabinet had been. 'Look,' he said.

Annie looked and saw what had grabbed their attention. A square piece of wood with a small hole for a handle and hinges along the opposite side.

'A trap door,' Ben whispered, and Joseph nodded his agreement.

Chapter Nine

'What is it, Joseph?'

Ben asked the question carefully, quietly. He was afraid to shatter the sudden calm that seemed to have descended upon the old man.

Joseph turned to look at him. His face was dirty, and Ben noticed a small cut on his left cheek, which bled slightly into his wiry grey stubble. 'What did you say your name was?' he demanded hoarsely.

Ben moistened his dry, dusty lips with his tongue. 'Ben,' he replied. 'Ben Tracey. And this is my cousin, Annie. You gave us a bit of a fright out there, you know.' The bombs might have stopped, but Ben still felt as though he needed to tiptoe around him.

Joseph inclined his head. 'Frights aren't always a bad thing, young man,' he whispered.

Ben's eyes narrowed. He seemed almost like a

different person now, calmer, more focused, somehow less, well, crazy.

'But you're right,' he continued. 'It was dangerous and I apologize for my behaviour. Sometimes I am not the master of my actions.' His eyes flickered back towards the trap door, and he stepped tentatively towards it. 'You are the bird-watcher, yes?'

'Sort of. It's more Annie, really . . .' His voice trailed off.

'There used to be a great many birds here when I was a young man. And other wildlife too. I used to walk out and watch them. When I first came here there would be huge fields of roe deer. And there were butterflies too, like you never saw. Fragile and colourful.'

Ben and Annie listened to him in edgy silence. There was something fragile about him too.

'The world of nature can be cruel, but not as cruel as the world of men,' the old man said. 'And I meant what I said, about Spadeadam. This is not a place for you to be wandering around. You should leave now.'

'He's right, Ben,' Annie piped up. 'Come on, we had an agreement. Let's get out of here.'

Ben nodded. He felt suddenly exhausted after everything that had just happened, and not in the mood to argue. 'Are you going to come with us, Joseph?' he asked.

Joseph shook his head. 'They'll come for me soon enough,' he said obscurely.

'Come for you? Who'll come for you?'

Joseph's head seemed to shake of its own accord, and for a moment Ben thought he saw a hint of the old craziness in his eyes. 'It's not important. But there are things I have to do before then. Things I have to see.'

'And this is one of them, right?'

The old man stared directly at Ben. His piercing green eyes seemed an alarming contrast to the crimson of the blood on his cheek. 'Right,' he said.

And then, as if they were no longer in the room, Joseph bent down and tried to lift up the trap door. It was heavy – too heavy for the old man – and the wooden square slipped from his hands, sending an echoing bang around the concrete walls.

Ben and Annie exchanged a long look as Joseph tried again, without success.

Ben sighed. He wanted to get out of there, but he couldn't bear to see the old man struggling. 'Here,' he said. 'I'll help you.'

Joseph turned round. 'You should leave,' he repeated, but he didn't decline the offer of help as Ben stepped forward. Together they heaved the trap door up onto its edge, then stepped back.

A musty, damp smell wafted up from the cellar below. It was the smell of darkness, disuse and age. A flight of steps, chipped and dusty, descended into the gloom – Ben could not see the bottom, nor indeed more than a couple of metres down, and he had the impression that nobody had opened up this cellar for a very, very long time.

As if in a trance, Joseph took a step down.

'Wait!' Ben said, and the old man looked sharply at him. 'You can't go down there in the pitch-dark.' He pulled his rucksack from his back, rummaged around and took out his torch. 'Here,' he said, handing it to Joseph.

The old man nodded gratefully; then, shining the torch downwards into the darkness, he descended.

Ben watched him disappear. He seemed so confident, considering the fact that minutes ago he had appeared to be barely on the edges of sanity. What was down there? What was he so sure he was going to find? Why was he prepared to take such risks to locate this place? Half of Ben wanted to follow him, to find out what was going on; the other half just wanted to get out of there.

'Ben!' Annie's voice disturbed his thoughts. 'Ben, we can't stay here.' But then her voice changed. 'Ben – *what's that noise?*'

He blinked. Sure enough, the familiar drone had started up in the distance.

It was getting louder.

And louder.

'Ben!' Annie screamed. 'They're back!' And as she

spoke, their ears filled with thunder, followed by the most spectacular crash they had yet heard. The walls of the hut seemed to shake – it was obvious that a bomb had just landed *very* near to them. And as though they had come out of nowhere, the air outside seemed suddenly to be filled yet again with the roar of jet engines.

Ben and Annie spun round to the open door in unison, just as it rattled on its hinges and debris flew into the hut. 'We can't go out there!' Annie shouted, and Ben knew she was right. But if one of those bombs hit the hut, it would be the end.

He grabbed her by the arm and pulled her towards the trap door. 'Come on!' he shouted. 'Down here!'

Hurriedly they started descending the steps.

As soon as they were below the level of the floor, Ben became aware of a chill. He shuddered. Below them he could see the torch, its beam moving around whatever was down there like a firefly, and faintly illuminating the figure of the strange old man holding it. The smell was even stronger down here, and in addition to the musty aroma of age there was something else. Something foul, as if things had been living and dying down here. What it was, Ben didn't even want to think. Under ordinary circumstances that smell would have made him turn round without a moment's thought. But this was not an ordinary situation. Planes were still flying overhead, and they could be victim to one of their devastating bombs any second. Whether they were safer down here, he couldn't say; but it surely couldn't be more dangerous.

The steps went a good way down – maybe five metres, maybe ten, Ben couldn't really tell in the darkness and in the hurry. At the bottom there seemed to be a kind of corridor. The felt their way along it, moving blindly and with care as they were unable to see where they were stepping. All they could do was make for the silhouetted figure of Joseph up ahead.

As he walked, Ben felt an irritating, tickling sensation against his face. It made him want to sneeze, but for some reason he felt he didn't want to make any sudden noises down here. The further they walked, the worse it got. Cobwebs, he thought to himself, as he brushed the silky strands away from his skin. He tried not to think of the spiders that had spun them. 'You all right?' he asked Annie.

'Not really,' Annie replied in a small voice. 'I don't like it down here.'

'It'll be OK,' he reassured her, though in truth he had to agree with her. His hand brushed against the wall – it felt cold to the touch, and damp. He wondered how long it had been since anybody else had touched that wall, and he tried not to think of the smell, which was getting worse and worse.

After several paces Ben sensed that the corridor was

opening out a little, until finally they stood side by side with Joseph in a low-ceilinged room. The stench was even stronger here – a gagging stink – and Ben found himself breathing through his mouth so that he didn't get too much of that putrid smell.

The old man held the torch above his shoulder and slowly scanned the beam of light around the room, meaning that Ben was only able to piece his surroundings together gradually. The walls were hung with what looked like metal medicine cabinets. Mostly they were closed, but a few of them had their doors hanging off where the hinges had rusted away, and these ones seemed to be empty. A bare wire hung from the ceiling. There was a metal trolley – it was difficult to see in the darkness, but it appeared to be thick with cobwebs and discoloured by rust – and next to the trolley was a chair. When Joseph's light fell upon it, he did not seem inclined to move the torch, deciding instead to stare at that chair. It seemed to be bolted firmly to the ground, and it too was made of metal: metal feet, metal arms, a metal back. Whoever had designed that chair had not intended it to be comfortable. It had some other purpose.

What that purpose was, though, Ben did not give much thought, because there was something else on his mind. A scurrying, scratching sound of something surprised by the light and the sudden company.

'Can you hear what I can hear, Ben?' Annie whispered.

'Yeah,' he replied. He didn't want to think about what it was that they had disturbed in the darkness, but he knew it was better to try and find out. 'Joseph,' he said. 'I think you'd better give me that torch.'

But the old man was still pointing the beam of light at the metal chair. 'This is it,' he said quietly, his voice strangely devoid of any emotion. 'This is it. I've been wanting to find this place for fifty years.'

'Honestly, Joseph. Give me the torch.'

'They've been telling me I imagined it. *For fifty years they've been telling me I imagined it.*' His voice betrayed a tremor now. 'I knew they were wrong. I always knew they were wrong.'

The scurrying grew more pronounced. With a shock that made him jolt his whole body, Ben felt something brush against his leg. Almost without thinking he shot his arm out and grabbed the torch from Joseph's hand. He took a deep breath and shone it down on the floor.

And the floor seemed to move as he did so.

Ben closed his eyes. If there was one thing he couldn't bear, it was these. 'Rats,' he whispered.

There were hundreds of them – at least that was what it looked like. He tried not to look at the tails – long, thick, glossy whips at least the same length as the rats' bodies, the very thought of which made him shiver. As he shone the torch down onto the floor, they parted like the Red Sea, but they soon grew used to the new sensation of the light, and started to swarm around the trio. Annie clutched onto Ben's arm so tightly it hurt. 'I think we should get out of here,' she said, her voice tight.

'Yeah,' Ben replied tensely. 'And fast. Come on, Joseph.'

But as he turned, Annie started screaming. Loudly. Hysterically. 'Get it off!' she yelled. '*It's on me. Get it off!*'

Ben spun round and shone the torch in her direction. Annie was looking, aghast, down at her legs, where a large black rat, its thick greasy tail writhing behind it, had attached itself by its claws to the material of her combat trousers. Several other rodents were gathered around by her boots. 'Get it off me!' she screamed again.

Every inch of Ben's body was repelled by the sight of the rat, but he knew he had to do something. The torch was still in his hand, and it felt like a good weight, so he struck the rat a solid blow on the side of its body. The rodent squealed, and fell with a heavy thump to the floor, where its sudden arrival dispersed its companions.

But not for long.

Ben felt the unmistakable scratching of tiny claws up

his legs and the horrible heaviness of something on his trousers. He knocked the rat down: as he did so, he felt his skin brush against the fur of the rodent that was scampering up him, and once more he found himself unable to restrain a shudder. Horrific memories of the rats he had encountered during the London floods came to his mind. He hated these creatures – why did they always seem to like him so much?

From somewhere deep inside his horror he became aware that Annie was screaming again; and even Joseph now appeared to be moving. 'The rats are more frightened than us,' he heard himself saying tersely, more to calm himself down than anything else. It wasn't much comfort, and the three of them started hurrying back towards the stairs, their feet occasionally knocking against a squeaking rat and the skin on their faces brushing against the cobwebs.

Ben couldn't tell whose feet it was he tripped over, but somewhere along the corridor he fell. He shouted out hoarsely, and tried to ignore the fact that the floor seemed to be undulating with shuffling furry bodies. There was a sudden troubled squeaking, and he pulled his hand quickly up off the ground when he realized it was resting on a strong, thick rat's tail. He shouted out again, his head suddenly swimming with panic as he tried to stumble to his feet. All strength seemed to have left him, however, and as the rats continued to swarm round his body, the walls started closing in on him. Claustrophobic. Surrounded by a sea of whip-like tails and stinking fur.

And then there was a hand on his arm. It was Joseph, pulling him up. 'On your feet, lad,' he said sternly, and that was all the instruction Ben needed. He pushed the panic from his mind and thrust himself up.

'Let's go,' he said with determination.

It was with unspeakable relief that Ben saw the dim light from the trap door illuminate the steps; and with even more relief that he heard no planes overhead. He stepped to one side to let the terrified Annie pass. Once she was on the steps, it was Joseph's turn. 'You go first, lad,' he said breathlessly, and Ben nodded, emerging back into the concrete hut with an explosive breath of air.

Annie's whole body was shuddering, and she was breathing in short, sudden gasps that would have been cries if there had been tears in her eyes. 'I – I don't care what's happening out there,' she stammered. 'There's no way I'm going back down those stairs.'

Ben's teeth were chattering as he nodded his head. He started drawing deep breaths to calm himself down, and for a few seconds the three of them stood by the trap door in silence.

It was Annie who spoke first. 'Er, do you mind if we

close that thing? I'm sure I can still hear those horrible rats.'

Ben nodded curtly, stepped round to the side of the opening and slammed the door shut. It echoed round the hut like a gunshot, and again the trio fell silent.

'So,' Ben said finally, more for the sake of putting the thought of the rats from his mind, 'fifty years, eh, Joseph? Can't think why you didn't go back there sooner.'

The old man turned to look at him. His grizzled face was serious, and he ignored Ben's ill-judged attempt at humour – an attempt that he instantly regretted the moment he caught that glance.

'*Rattus norvegicus,*' he said. 'The brown rat. Coarse hair, average body weight of three hundred and fifty grams. Acute hearing, sensitive to ultrasound. Selectively bred as laboratory rats for medical experimentation, which means that their presence down there is more apt than you could ever imagine.' Joseph's lip curled into a frown. 'You don't understand, lad,' he continued in a low voice. 'It's OK – there's no reason why you should. But what happened down there fifty years ago was far worse than anything you've seen today.' His green eyes fixed themselves on Ben, who found that he was unable to look away, so commanding was that gaze.

Ben heard his own heart beating as the two of them stared intently at each other.

'I'm sorry,' Ben said finally. 'I didn't mean to—'

'Just go,' Joseph interrupted. 'Get out. Get away.' He turned, releasing Ben from his fearsome gaze.

Ben nodded, then looked towards Annie. 'Come on,' he said. 'I think we should go home.'

'That's the most sensible thing you've said all day,' she replied. They turned their back on Joseph and walked towards the door. Ben gave the old man one last glance over his shoulder. He was looking around the hut again, that same inscrutable expression on his face.

Ben's eyes, unused to the brightness of the outside, smarted slightly as he walked into the daylight, so he covered them briefly with his hand. So it was that Annie saw them first – Ben heard her gasp even before he noticed them, and he felt her grasp his arm. But when he removed his hands from over his eyes, he stopped dead in his tracks.

There must have been five or six of them, grim-faced RAF men in combat fatigues and military berets, surrounding the hut. They were all heavily armed with ugly, black service rifles, and each of the guns was pointed directly at Ben and Annie.

'Hit the floor!' one of the soldiers barked. 'Lie on the floor with your hands on your head! Get down! Get down or we shoot!'

Chapter Ten

Ben hit the dirt. Next to him, he sensed Annie doing the same.

'Get your hands on your head!' he heard the soldier shout, and he did as he was told. He felt his rucksack being grabbed from him, then his wrists being roughly seized and pulled down behind his back, where one of their captors clunked a pair of metal handcuffs on him.

'Who else was in there with you?' a voice barked.

'Only one person,' Ben replied through gritted teeth. The gravel-strewn ground scratched against his cheek as he spoke. 'He's an old man. His name's Joseph and he's pretty frail. Go easy on him.' He watched as three sets of heavy-booted feet rushed past his field of vision. 'He's not armed,' Ben shouted. 'He's harmless—'

But the soldiers were already shouting, 'Get to the floor! Get to the floor!'

From inside the hut, Ben heard Joseph's distinctive voice. 'I'm an old man,' he said calmly. 'You are three heavily armed soldiers. It's unlikely I'm going to overcome you with my bare hands, don't you think?'

Instantly there was a sickening thump, like the butt of a rifle against skin and bone, and then the unmistakable sound of Joseph groaning and falling to the floor. 'Leave him alone!' Ben shouted, before being unceremoniously pulled to his feet, as was Annie. They watched as the old man, a large welt already visible on the side of his face, was dragged out of the hut. One of the soldiers struck him harshly in the pit of his stomach. He fell to his knees before his arms were grabbed behind his back and he too was restrained with cuffs.

Nearby there was a military vehicle – a large, canvas-covered four by four. Wordlessly they were pushed towards the truck and bundled into the back, while three soldiers, their weapons still firmly in their fists, joined them to keep guard. The back of the truck was pulled closed, and it started moving slowly along the rough dirt track.

The atmosphere was tense. The bruise on Joseph's face seemed to be getting darker by the minute; Annie kept looking at it, and then furiously back at the soldiers. Ben could tell that she was fuming that an RAF soldier should have inflicted such a wound on an unarmed old man. Finally one of the soldiers – a burly man with a nose that looked like it had been broken at some stage in the past – spoke. 'Pretty stupid place for a couple of kids to be hanging out,' he told them. He directed his attention towards Joseph. 'But I might have expected something a bit more sensible from an old boy like you.'

Joseph's face remained stony. 'Stupidity isn't just for young people,' he said quietly, touching his fingers to his bruised face as if to illustrate his point.

The soldier sneered.

'Where are you taking us?' Annie demanded.

'Same place we take everyone caught interfering in military operations,' he replied dismissively. 'To a holding cell, while we evaluate whether or not you're a threat to national security.'

'National security!' Annie blustered. 'That's ridiculous.'

The soldier stretched out his arm and grabbed Annie firmly by the face, pinching her cheeks. 'I'll tell you what,' he said in a low growl. 'How about you shut up, and I'll see to it that you don't end up like your old friend there.'

The other two soldiers sniggered at his comment.

Annie's lips thinned; Ben prayed that she would just keep quiet, but he knew how likely that was. 'You should be ashamed of yourself,' she spat at the soldier.

'You're a disgrace to the uniform, and when I next speak to my father—'

'Annie, no!' Ben interrupted her.

'Shut up, Ben. When I next speak to my father, he's going to hear about this.'

The soldier grinned at his colleagues. 'Any particular reason why we should be running scared from your daddy?'

'Well,' Annie replied. 'That all depends on your rank, doesn't it?'

The soldier's eyes narrowed. 'Flight lieutenant,' he said cautiously.

'Right,' Annie smiled with satisfaction. 'Then he outranks you by four rungs.'

The soldier looked like he was working that out in his head. 'Your dad's an air commodore?' he asked.

'Yeah,' said Annie, 'and I think he'll have something to say about the way you treated Joseph, don't you?'

But the flight lieutenant didn't seem to be listening. Instead he stood up and, keeping his free hand against the side of the truck to steady himself as they continued down the bumpy road, he knocked the butt of his rifle against the cab. Three times. A clear, measured signal, and the truck trundled to a halt. The three soldiers sat exchanging nervous glances while they waited for the two in the front to open the back.

'What is it?' the soldier who seemed to be in charge asked impatiently.

'The girl,' replied the flight lieutenant. 'She says her father's an air commodore.'

The soldiers fell silent, clearly digesting this information. As they did, Ben found himself looking from face to face. When his gaze finally fell on the other soldier standing outside the truck, he blinked.

He recognized that face. He had seen him somewhere before.

'Change of plan,' the leader barked, interrupting Ben's thoughts. 'We'll take them to the doc.'

The flight lieutenant looked troubled. 'The doc? Are you sure that's a good idea, sir.'

'We haven't got any choice. He can decide what to do next. And this thing will be over in twenty-four hours, and by that time we'll all be out of the country.'

'But, sir—'

'It's an order, soldier,' the leader barked, and he slammed the back of the truck shut. From outside, Ben heard the leader talk to the soldier he recognized. 'Take us there,' he said. 'And make sure we're not followed.'

Seconds later, they were moving again.

'Where are we going?' Annie asked the soldiers. She was unable to hide the nervousness in her voice.

The soldiers didn't answer – the arrogance seemed to have been kicked out of them by the curt words of their superior officer. Instead, they sat there quietly, exchanging the occasional nervous glance that did nothing for Ben's confidence in where all this was leading.

As they travelled, Ben did his best to pay attention to the twists and turns of their route. Why he did so he couldn't have said. They were in the custody of armed RAF soldiers, so any thoughts they might have of trying to escape and weave their way back to the outskirts of the base would be pretty ill-advised. But there was something about these guys that didn't ring true. 'What did he mean?' He asked the question out loud, but it was more to himself than anything else.

'Who?' the flight lieutenant said.

'Back then, when he said you'd all be out of the country.'

'Shut up,' he was told for the second time in the past few minutes.

They endured about twenty minutes of uncomfortable driving. Ben and Annie looked at each other nervously, and then over at Joseph, who was simply staring impassively against the opposite wall. As they drove, Ben found himself remembering the stark warning the old man had given the previous night. 'Strange things going on at Spadeadam.'

Too right, he thought to himself. Too right.

They came to a sudden stop: the doors opened and

the three soldiers jumped down. 'Get out,' the leader barked. Slowly, the handcuffed trio stood up and made their way down from the truck. The five soldiers were standing outside an old building – more of a shack really, made of wood stained dark with creosote. As they stood there brandishing their weapons, Ben sought out the face he recognized. There was no doubt about it – he had only caught a fleeting glimpse of the man, and even then from a distance, but he was absolutely sure he knew where he had seen him before. As if to confirm his suspicion, he saw that the man was carrying a rifle, unlike any of the other RAF soldiers he had seen.

'Shot any rare birds lately?' he asked the soldier, one eyebrow raised in ironic questioning.

The man's eyes narrowed. 'How—?' he started to say, but the commanding officer interrupted him.

'Quiet, all of you.' He pointed at Joseph, Ben and Annie. 'You three, inside.'

Ben gave the soldiers a disparaging look, and they were hustled through the door, which was closed and locked behind them.

'This isn't right,' Annie let out explosively as soon as they were alone. 'They're up to something. They'd never—'

'I know,' interrupted Ben sharply. And then, more soothingly, 'I know.'

Annie breathed in deeply. 'You sure that was him – the one who shot the hen harrier?'

'Positive,' Ben replied. 'Absolutely positive.'

The shack was dark, the only source of light being a small window in the side that was covered in a thick layer of greasy dust. Joseph stood at the window, looking out emotionlessly. He did not seem even remotely bothered by the bruising on his face – it was as though he didn't even feel it. 'Joseph,' Ben said, trying to get his attention.

The old man continued to stare out of the window.

'Joseph,' Ben repeated. 'You have to listen to me. Do you remember when we spoke last night?'

Slowly Joseph turned to look at him.

'You told me it was obvious why someone had been shooting birds round here. It's to keep *us* away, isn't it? People *like* us, I mean. There's something going on here and they don't want anyone snooping around.'

Joseph smiled at him, revealing his yellowing teeth. 'Well done, Ben,' he said quietly. 'It's good to see young minds working properly.' He turned to look back out of the window again. 'Wildlife was always a problem for them, even in the old days. Brought people to the area, you see. People like you. And the last thing they ever wanted was inquisitive minds lurking around, so they tried to keep the numbers of the rare animals down.'

'That cellar,' Annie asked. 'What is it? You said you'd

been looking for it. Why? Have you been there before?'

'Oh, yes,' Joseph replied, his voice little more than a whisper. 'I've been there before. Many, many years ago. That was where it all started for me. Or should I say, where it all ended.'

'What ended?'

Joseph turned back to look at her.

'My life,' he said.

Ben felt a chill descend. A million questions poured into his head – there was so much more to this strange old man than he had previously thought – and he barely knew where to begin. But he didn't even get a chance, because at that moment he heard the door open.

All three of them spun round nervously to see who was there.

The man who filled the doorway was not dressed in combat fatigues; instead he wore a thin brown suit and a black tie. He was old, at least as old as Joseph – indeed he did not look dissimilar. His hair was balding, he had round glasses and a short, neatly trimmed grey beard and his skin was deeply lined. Under his eyes were huge black bags that would have looked odd on any other face, but somehow, Ben thought, suited the funereal features of this stern-looking individual.

'Let us out of here!' he heard Annie demand.

But the man merely flicked his hand in Annie's

direction, as though swatting a fly. Instead, all his attention was focused on Joseph.

And Joseph stared back. There were a thousand unsaid things in that one stare, and it lasted for a long, long time.

The man took a step back and then turned to the soldier standing next to him. 'Take them over to the lab complex,' he said quietly. 'I'll head over there first while I decide what to do.' The soldier nodded, and shut the door, locking it behind him.

In the shack all was quiet. Joseph was still staring at the door as if he hadn't even noticed that it had been closed. For a full minute he stood there while Ben and Annie watched and then, almost imperceptibly at first but with gradually increasing vigour, he started to tremble. 'Still here,' he muttered under his breath. 'Still here.' He shook his head and started to look out of the window yet again.

A rushing urgency filled Ben. Who was the man? Had Joseph recognized him? Could he shed some sort of light on what was going on here? For all his need to understand, however, he sensed that now, of all times, Joseph had to be dealt with sensitively. He could tell Annie felt the same – she was staring at the old man with wide eyes of sympathy.

Ben approached Joseph and stood next to him. 'Are you all right, Joseph?' he asked.

'Still here,' he muttered again. 'I'd never have thought that *he'd* still be here.'

Ben swallowed nervously. 'Do you know him, Joseph?'

The old man turned to look imperiously down at him, and for the first time Ben became aware of just how tall he was. 'Of course I know him, lad,' Joseph replied in a whisper.

His eyes flicked towards the door once more, then back to Ben.

'Of course I know him. His name is Doctor Lucian Sinclair. He's my brother.'

Chapter Eleven

As Joseph spoke, the door opened again. The flight lieutenant walked in, gun at the ready, followed by two of his colleagues. They each carried rough strips of cloth that looked as if they had just been hurriedly ripped from one of the soldier's articles of clothing.

'Blindfold them,' the flight lieutenant said.

'Don't you dare,' Annie started to say with fire in her voice. 'Give me my rucksack. I want my phone – I demand to make a phone call.'

'Shut up,' the flight lieutenant growled, just as Ben felt himself being grabbed by one of the soldiers. He struggled, kicking his heel hard into the man's shin. His captor shouted out, but didn't let go. With his hands restrained by the cuffs and the fact that the RAF man was too strong for him, Ben soon had the rough cloth firmly tied around his eyes. As the blackness engulfed him, he sensed Annie scuffling ineffectually; Joseph, however, seemed to accept what was happening and was blindfolded without complaint.

Once the blindfolds had been applied, Ben was hustled out of the shack and felt himself being pushed up into the truck yet again. The doors slammed shut and the vehicle started to move. It was difficult to tell in the darkness who else was in the truck with them, but he could only assume that the same three soldiers who had accompanied them before were there, so he knew he could not discuss escape plans or other theories in front of them. And so the trio kept quiet, disorientated by the blindfolds and the constant bumping of the truck over difficult roads. Before long it became clear to Ben that even if they managed to get away, it wouldn't make any difference: they would be totally lost.

All sense of time seemed to be confused, so Ben had no idea how long they drove for. Finally, however, they came to an abrupt stop and once more they were man-handled off the truck.

'Get them down there,' the voice of the leader said curtly.

Someone pushed Ben from behind. 'Hey,' he complained as he stumbled forward. The moment he spoke, however, he felt someone deal him a crushing blow in the stomach. He doubled over, winded, falling to the ground, where he felt his knees rustle in a patch of fallen leaves.

'Get up,' someone told him, and he was pulled gasping to his feet before being dragged through another door. 'Steps,' his aggressive companion murmured to him, and sure enough Ben found himself walking down a flight of stairs. For some reason – he didn't know why – he found himself counting them. Fifteen, twenty, twenty-five, twenty-six – they were going some way underground. He found himself praying that they wouldn't see any more rats down here.

'Where are you taking us?' he demanded; but he was not favoured with a reply. Just another push that forced him down a narrow corridor – his uneven gait meant he occasionally brushed against the wall on either side, and he could tell that those walls were closer together than made him entirely comfortable. The corridor seemed to wind round erratically; occasionally they would take a left or a right turn. Ben felt as though he was in some kind of fiendish underground maze, and he knew he had no chance of getting back to the entrance unless he had a great deal of luck.

Abruptly they came to a stop. There was the sound of somebody knocking on a door, and then of the door opening. They were pushed inside. 'Johnson,' a quiet voice said, 'you stay here. The rest of you, leave us.'

There was a shuffling of feet as the soldiers left the room.

Silence. A thick, meaningful silence that seemed to stick to them. And then the quiet voice spoke again.

'You really should have stayed away, Joseph.'

Ben heard Joseph take a deep breath. When he spoke, it was with a clarity that might not have been expected of him. 'Stayed away, Lucian? I rather think you should not have sent me away in the first place.'

'It was for your own good,' Lucian replied sharply.

A pause. '*My* own good?' Joseph asked him, his voice calm. 'Or yours?'

Lucian breathed out with a heavy snort. 'I wouldn't expect you to understand. Science requires a clear mind – not something you were ever blessed with.'

Ben waited for a response from Joseph, but there was none.

When Lucian spoke again, his voice had calmed. 'How convenient,' he almost purred, 'that you should turn up now of all times.'

Ben sensed him walking thoughtfully among the silent trio.

'All I need to know, Joseph, is what you have heard and who you have heard it from.'

'You're as mistaken as you ever were, Lucian,' Joseph said, his voice cracking a bit. 'I don't know what it is that you've got going on here, and frankly I don't care.

I came to Spadeadam to reassure myself that I've not been deceiving myself these last fifty years. I've done that beyond question, so why don't you just let us all go?'

Lucian seemed to contemplate that for a moment. 'You never were a good liar, Joseph,' he commented finally. 'Who are your two friends? They're a little young for heroics, aren't they? It was stupid of you to bring them.'

'He didn't!' Ben interrupted defiantly. 'We came here by ourselves.'

He had barely finished speaking when he felt a hand at his face. With a sudden yank, the blindfold was ripped roughly from around his head, and Ben was face to face with Joseph's brother, able to look at him properly. He still wore the same thin brown suit as when they had first seen him, but it was his be-spectacled face that interested Ben. Now he knew that Lucian and Joseph were brothers, he could see the resemblance. There was not the same hooked nose or floppy hair, but something around the mouth was similar, as were the eyes – now half closed in an expression of the deepest mistrust. 'You must think I'm stupid, you idiot child,' he hissed. 'But let me tell you this. I've been working on Vortex for nearly as long as you've been alive, and if you think I'm going to let you three interfere with it now, then you've got another think coming. It will be delivered tomorrow, there will be no trace of its development here and the few of us who know about it will be on a plane out of the country with enough money to fade into obscurity.'

He strode up to Annie, removed her blindfold, and then did the same to Joseph. It was to his brother that he spoke next. 'History will not remember the name of the person who bestowed this gift upon it,' he said, 'but that does not matter. I am willing to sacrifice my own fame for the greater good.'

Joseph looked flatly at him. 'For the greater good, Lucian? It strikes me that I've heard you say that once before, a long time ago.'

Lucian's lip curled. 'You never did understand, Joseph.' He turned to the flight lieutenant. 'We need to keep them out of the way until tomorrow and make sure that none of our *colleagues*' – he spoke the word with a certain amount of distaste – 'above ground start asking questions about them. You're sure we picked them up before their presence was noticed? And no one saw you move them in or out of the truck earlier?'

'We're sure,' Johnson replied.

'Good,' Lucian replied. He turned to look back at the trio. 'Flight Lieutenant Johnson will accompany you to a secure unit while I decide exactly what to do with you.' He stared directly at Joseph. 'Take a good look at my face, brother,' he said quietly. 'It's the last time you'll ever see it.'

Joseph stared back at him, gazing into his brother's eyes, his own face unreadable. 'Shall we go, Flight Lieutenant?' he asked gently. He did not see Lucian nod his approval, because he was resolutely looking the other way.

Lieutenant Colonel Oleg Kasparov of the Russian army watched the sun setting over the Spadeadam marshland. The insects had descended in force as dusk arrived, and a bite on his left hand irritated him, but he neither scratched it nor complained. Beside him in the back of the car was his host for the duration of his visit, a pleasant and enthusiastic wing commander by the name of Stevens who had no idea that Kasparov's official visit to Spadeadam was nothing more than a front for some very *un*official business. And now that his two aides had been dismissed, he could get on with that business.

'It's great to have you here, Lieutenant Colonel,' he was saying politely. 'Good to be able to show you guys round what we do here after so many years of cold war.'

Kasparov nodded abruptly. 'The Russian army is grateful to you for your hospitality.' He did his best to hide a rare smile. This enthusiastic British officer could never guess that the gratitude of the Russian military was the furthest thing from his mind. He had a new paymaster now, and an ulterior motive for being at the RAF base at that time. If he made sure everything ran smoothly, the Russian oligarch from whom he now took his orders would make him rich – rich enough to leave the army and never work again.

The car pulled to a halt outside a row of modern brick buildings. 'These will be your lodgings,' Stevens said as the driver walked round and opened the door for Kasparov. 'I trust you'll find them comfortable.'

'I'm sure I will,' Kasparov replied, shaking Stevens's outstretched hand, then hauling his large-framed body out of the car and picking up the bag that the driver had fetched from the boot. 'Until tomorrow morning, Wing Commander.'

'Tomorrow morning,' Stevens replied, and the car drove off.

Kasparov walked up to the door of his lodgings and stepped inside. He barely noticed the clean, comfortable surroundings; he simply dropped the bag in the hallway and pulled his mobile phone from the pocket of his military jacket, then dialled the number he had been given.

'It is Kasparov,' he said curtly when his call was answered. 'I am ready to be collected.' He flicked the phone shut and walked into the front room.

It was dark in there, but he didn't bother to switch

the light on. Instead he stood at the window and looked out over the wide expanse of countryside ahead of him, silently contemplating what he had to do. A group of renegade North Korean politicians were furious that their leader appeared to be losing his ambition for military supremacy. They had won his boss's little auction for the weapon this scientist had been developing without the knowledge of his RAF employers. It was Kasparov's job to check that everything was as it should be before the Vortex device was finally delivered. Once that happened, he could return to Russia, resign his commission and head straight to the little *dacha* in the countryside where he could allow himself time to decide how to spend his life and his money.

Gradually he became aware of headlamps in the distance. They grew hypnotically closer as Kasparov watched them impassively. Only when they were really quite near did he move. He walked out of the front door and waited for the car to stop.

When it did, another RAF soldier stepped out of it.

'Lieutenant Colonel Kasparov?'

'Flight Lieutenant Johnson?'

Johnson nodded. 'You have a coat?'

Kasparov shook his head. 'I am used to the Russian winter,' he said scornfully. 'I will not need a coat.'

Johnson shrugged. 'Whatever,' he said. 'Shall we go?'

'Yes,' Kasparov replied. 'We shall. I wish to see the

Vortex device as soon as possible. Take me there now.'

And without a further word, he stepped into the back of the car, waiting impatiently for Flight Lieutenant Johnson to do as he had instructed.

Chapter Twelve

Chin-Hwa slept. As he slept, he dreamed. And as he dreamed, he saw terrible things.

He saw the cities of the world, their streets full of panicked people. He saw the fear in their faces, and the chaos all around them. He saw lines of hospital beds, their occupants thin and gaunt – the unmistakable look of the dying. He saw burning fireballs in the air, and heard the screams of the aeroplane passengers as they fell to earth, and to their death. He saw nuclear missiles flying undetected towards the West, and he wondered whether their arrival might not be a blessed release to the people they were sent to destroy.

And he saw Vortex. Small. Silent. Lethal. It did not care whom it affected: men or women, adults or children – everyone's life would be destroyed.

He shouted out in his sleep and awoke sweating. It

took him a moment to realize that his dream had not been real, but in a way that was small comfort. It *could* be only too real, and very soon. And Chin-Hwa would have to take his share of the blame.

The meeting he'd had with the government men kept playing around in his head. London, New York, Los Angeles, Madrid. He never expected things to get this far. Vortex was just a deterrent. It was meant to keep the peace and stop the West from invading his country. No one ever intended to actually *use* it – at least that was what he'd been told. He was just being ordered to copy it. If he didn't do it, someone else would.

But as he dressed and stomped around his sparse apartment, he imagined more of the devastation the weapon could inflict on those major cities. He imagined the chaos. He imagined the death, the destruction. He told himself that it was not *his* fault. This would have gone ahead without him. And if he hadn't complied – his eyes flicked over to the door of the bedroom in which his mother now slept, even though it was the middle of the day. She spent more and more time in bed now; but he knew the fact that she was frail would not stop the government stooges from carrying out their threat. He was doing the right thing, he told himself, in keeping his knowledge to himself.

But what would she say? What would she say if he

told her about Vortex and the terrible things it could do? And that thought led his eyes to fall upon a picture of his father. Ki-Woon had been a good man. Honest. Principled. Willing to die for what he believed in. He had told Chin-Hwa to look after his mother, but hadn't he himself followed his conscience all those years ago?

As he sat there, Chin-Hwa felt the absence of his father more bitterly than he ever had before. He would have known what to do. And Ki-Woon seemed to stare out of the picture at his son. 'Look into your heart, Chin-Hwa,' he seemed to say. 'Do what you think is right.'

In that moment Chin-Hwa knew he was fooling himself. All those times he had been brought into the government buildings and asked the same questions again and again. In his expert opinion, would Vortex work? Would it be effective over the range that was being claimed? Once they had their hands on the machinery, would he be able to copy it? Each time he had answered in the same way: the theory of Vortex was sound, but it would be a very difficult device to engineer. Yes, if they managed to engineer it, then the range was realistic. And yes, he would be able to copy it. He didn't really know if he could, but what else could he say?

And he had known, even then, that these shadowy government officials did not want Vortex simply as a deterrent.

They wanted it as an instrument of war.

Chin-Hwa understood how devastating it could be, and as he stared at his father's picture, he knew with a sudden clarity what he had to do. He knew he had to put things right.

He stood up abruptly and walked into the small kitchen. At the back of one of the almost empty cupboards there was a small box. He opened it and removed a thin wad of crumpled notes, money that he had saved over a long period of time in case of an emergency. Really he had been thinking about his mother needing medical care, but this, he realized, was a different kind of emergency. The *worst* kind of emergency. And if he did nothing to stop it, he would have only himself to blame.

Chin-Hwa walked to the window. It was still raining outside, and as he looked down the twenty storeys of the high-rise building in which he and his mother lived, he saw that the pavements were almost bare.

Almost, except for the one man in a heavy raincoat who was standing on the other side of the road. Standing and watching. Watching and waiting.

Chin-Hwa had become used to being followed. They were clever at it, never sending the same man twice so that he wouldn't recognize his pursuer, but he had become aware of it soon after that first meeting with the government men. Wherever he went there was

somebody nearby, as dependable as his own shadow.
Following. Watching. Sometimes Chin-Hwa would
play games with them, walking down a deserted side
street and then stopping to look back. His pursuers
would not try to hide. They would just stand there, still
and expressionless, then start following him again as
soon as he went on his way.

Today, though, he was going to have to lose him.

He stepped into the small bedroom where his
mother slept, bed-bound for most of her time now. 'I'm
going out,' he said softly, and was relieved to note that
she was asleep and so unable to question why he was
stepping outside in this rain. He grabbed his one coat
that he had to make do with, whatever the weather,
then left the flat.

There was only one way out of the apartment block,
and as soon as he descended the concrete stairwell and
stepped outside, he saw the man on the other side of
the road stand up a little straighter, then start to follow
him as he walked through the rain towards the tram
stop. He took the tram every day – like most North
Koreans he was too poor to own a car, and the
Pyongyang metro was too unreliable – and was used to
waiting at that little tram stop, his shadow never standing more than a few metres away.

By the time the orange and white tram trundled
along, Chin-Hwa was soaked to the skin. The doors

hissed open and he stepped up into the tram, closely followed by the man in the heavy coat, then shuffled halfway up the carriage to where there was another set of doors. He stood close by them, listening carefully for the telltale hiss that would indicate they were about to shut.

When the hiss came, he slipped outside again.

The doors shut firmly behind him, and as the tram moved off, he caught sight of his pursuer through the window, his expressionless face now marked with anger. Their gaze remained locked until the tram took him out of sight.

He hurried quickly in the other direction, knowing that the tram's next stop was not that far away, and his shadow would return here as soon as possible. But as he pattered down the street he became aware of something else.

Footsteps.

He looked over his shoulder and saw another rain-coat-clad man walking about ten metres behind him, clearly trying to keep up with Chin-Hwa's energetic pace. He had seen enough of these guys to know when he was being followed, but there had never been more than one of them before. He felt a sense of rising panic as he realized that the surveillance must have been increased very recently – since this morning, in fact – and he cursed himself for having asked too many questions in the government meeting.

He was followed all the way into the centre of Pyongyang. As he walked he desperately tried to think of a way to lose his shadow. There was no way he could pull the tram trick again; he *could* head for a metro station, but trains were unlikely to be running as it was not the rush hour. In the end, he headed for the huge white building of Department Store Number 1, one of the capital's biggest shops and a place he would never normally set foot. Maybe, just maybe, he could lose his trail here.

The store was not crowded. His clothes dripped onto the shiny floor as he walked past aisles of goods he could not afford – business suits in the menswear department, wooden machine guns in the toy area. All the while he kept checking over his shoulder; all the while he saw that the man in the heavy raincoat was following.

On a whim, he darted left, past a row of children's clothes that were all of an identical style. He swung round to his right, then to his left again. Ahead of him was a flight of steps. He ran to the stairs and thundered down them, then hurtled through a door and out into the street again where he ran with all the energy he had. As soon as he could make a turn off that road, he did; then he did all he could to lose himself in the unfamiliar streets. If he didn't know where he was, Chin-Hwa reasoned, then nor would his shadow.

Sure enough, when he looked back, there was no sign of him.

Chin-Hwa would pay for this, of that he was sure. Nobody could prove that he had lost his trail on purpose, but that didn't matter in North Korea. He'd be hauled in, questioned, maybe even tortured. Perhaps they would come for his mother. He couldn't think about all that, though. If he did, it would distract him from what he had to do. And he knew what that was.

There was only one Internet café in Pyongyang, and that had recently opened. It was never full, however, because the price of half an hour on the computers cost more than most Koreans earned in a month. It was really just for foreign visitors, and to present the image of North Korea being a modern state, even though only a tiny fraction of the population had ever used it.

When Chin-Hwa walked in, he attracted strange looks; they became even stranger when he pulled his wad of damp notes from out of his sopping pockets and handed them to the man in charge, who counted them out carefully. Warily, he was shown to a computer terminal. 'Half an hour,' he was told curtly.

Chin-Hwa nodded. Half an hour to save the world. It didn't seem like long. He put his fingers to the keyboard and started typing.

Chapter Thirteen

The cell in which Ben, Annie and Joseph found themselves was empty apart from a flickering strip light on the ceiling and a metal plate by heavy electric doors that had hissed firmly shut when they had been unceremoniously thrown in here. Flight Lieutenant Johnson had at least removed the handcuffs that were by now cutting into the skin around their wrists, but then he had left them without a word.

There were no windows in the cell – just concrete walls – and in the weak artificial light it was impossible to judge how much time was passing. Joseph had walked to the far corner of the cell, sat down and huddled his arms around his knees; Annie, on the other hand, was pacing up and down, fuming. 'What's going on here?' she demanded of nobody in particular. 'I don't understand. What's Vortex? Why are we being held?'

She turned to Ben and pointed a slightly threatening finger at him. 'If you try and tell me that these people are doing this with the full knowledge of the RAF—'

Ben raised his hand to quieten her. 'I don't think that, Annie,' he said softly. 'Of course I don't think that.' He looked meaningfully over at Joseph, then back at Annie, who closed her eyes for a moment, took a deep breath and then gave him a nod. Together they approached the old man, who was still sitting in the corner, staring impassively into the middle distance. Ben felt a bit uncomfortable, towering over someone so much older than him.

'I think we need to talk, Joseph,' he said quietly. 'I think you need to tell us what's going on. What was your brother talking about? When were you sent away? What's Vortex? Why are you here?'

Joseph looked slowly up at them. His eyes were faintly bloodshot and his floppy hair straggled over his face.

'You'll have to excuse me,' he replied, his voice hoarse. 'It has been rather a shock for me to see my brother again after so many years. I never thought he would still be here. I thought he would have settled into a quiet retirement. It seems I was very wrong.'

'Joseph,' Ben insisted urgently, 'I think we're in danger. You *got* to tell us what's going on.'

'Danger?' Joseph replied with a sinister little chuckle.

'Oh, we're in danger, all right. There's no doubt about that. I told you to stay away from this place.'

'Yeah, well we didn't,' Ben answered him shortly.

Joseph smiled. 'No,' he said. 'You didn't.' He tapped the cold concrete floor where he was sitting. 'I suppose you'd better both sit down. It's a complicated story.'

Ben and Annie exchanged a glance, then did as they were told.

'My brother Lucian is two years older than me,' he began. 'When we were young, we both followed the path of the sciences. We were both physicists. That's how we ended up working here.'

'At Spadeadam, you mean?' Ben asked.

'Yes. At Spadeadam.' Joseph's eyes misted over. 'It was like a magnet for scientists in the late nineteen fifties. They were developing the Blue Streak missile, and there was a real outlet for our skills, and a chance for us to learn.'

'But there was more going on here than just Blue Streak, wasn't there?' Ben asked intuitively.

'Oh, yes,' Joseph replied. 'A great deal more. It was all top secret, of course. It had to be – this was not the sort of science that anyone wanted to become public knowledge. And it was the sort of thing to which Lucian was bound to be attracted. He was never comfortable with the fact that – forgive me for saying it – his younger brother was a more natural scientist. He was attracted towards realms of scientific endeavour that he knew I would go nowhere near.'

Ben found he was holding his breath. 'Like what?' he asked.

Joseph shrugged. 'Certain areas of weapons research, for one.'

'But . . .' Annie faltered slightly. 'There's nothing wrong with that, is there? I mean, everyone researches new weapons, don't they? It's not like we go to war in Spitfires any more.'

Joseph's bloodshot eyes fixed Annie with a piercing stare. 'You are too young to remember Hiroshima,' he said starkly, and Annie fell silent.

'In any case,' Joseph continued, 'I don't believe we are talking about the same kind of weapons research. The experimentation that was being done here fifty years ago would have been repellent even to you, my dear.'

Ben sensed Annie flushing with embarrassment.

'I admit,' the old man said, 'that perhaps I am as guilty as anyone. I worked on Blue Streak. I helped develop missiles. But Lucian' – and here Joseph shook his head sadly – 'got wind of other experiments being conducted in secret, in underground laboratories much like the ones we are in now. Experiments involving human subjects.'

Ben and Annie looked aghast at him.

'Mostly they used criminals,' Joseph carried on regardless of their evident horror. 'The men in grey suits offered them shorter sentences in return for their permission to let people like Lucian treat them as if they were little more than laboratory rats. My brother was always interested in the effects of electrical stimuli on the human brain, and here he was given free rein to conduct his loathsome research without any thought for what he was doing to the poor people who had unwittingly volunteered themselves.'

Ben's eyes narrowed as he listened to what Joseph had to say. Men in grey suits? Evil scientists? Human experiments? It all sounded a bit far-fetched to him, like the conspiracy theories he had read about on the Internet. But then he looked around, reminding himself that he was currently trapped in a concrete cell far underground during what was supposed to be a pleasant bird-watching holiday. More than that, there was something in Joseph's voice that had the desperate ring of truth.

'But that's not weapons research,' he heard Annie saying, the shock in her voice clear to hear.

'Really?' Joseph asked. 'Weapons come in many forms. Some of them we deem to be acceptable, others we don't. Lucian boasted to me that he was developing ways of forcing prisoners of war to give us information we might want. He boasted that he and his associates were close to being able to alter the memories of enemy forces – real psychological warfare.'

'Why did he tell you all this, if he knew you didn't approve?' Ben asked.

'I don't know,' Joseph replied. 'Pride, I suppose. Perhaps it made him feel good to be in the know about something. And of course, he thought he had some sort of hold over me now.'

'I don't understand,' Annie asked. 'Why?'

Joseph looked at the two of them in turn. There was a sadness around his eyes now, as though telling them all this had drained him emotionally.

'Lucian and his associates tried to manipulate their subjects' mental states to alter brain function, using electrical and chemical means. But you can't just attach an electrode to someone's head, or pump them full of drugs, and expect them to lose all their mental faculties. These techniques only really work to their full effect if there is already a history of mental deficiency in the subject. Lucian was trying to scare me, because he knew that I had a history of mild mental illness.'

Ben and Annie remained quiet, not knowing what to say.

The old man continued. 'Lucian knew that I would not approve of what was going on, but it was clear what he was threatening me with.'

Annie's eyes were glassy now, as though she were fighting back tears. 'But he's your brother,' she whispered.

Joseph nodded.

'What did you do?' Ben asked.

It took a while for Joseph to reply, as though he were reliving the events that followed next. When he finally spoke, it was in a slow, measured tone of voice. 'Scientists have a duty,' he said firmly. 'A morality. Just because we *can* do something, it doesn't mean that we *should*.' He looked sharply at Ben and Annie. 'I went to Lucian. I begged him to stop doing what he was doing. And when he refused, I told him that I was going to blow the whistle on his activities.'

Silence.

'He said I was naïve. Thinking back, he was probably right. I have no doubt that their experiments were being carried out with the full knowledge of the British intelligence services, and any attempts I made to reveal them would have been firmly stamped on. But I had to do something, and so I stood firm and insisted that I would go to the authorities.'

'But you never did, did you?' asked Ben, his voice little more than a whisper.

Joseph smiled sadly and shook his head. 'They came for me just before morning – Lucian and his colleague, his boss really, who specialized in chemical mind control. They bundled me into the back of a military vehicle and took me to an underground bunker they had reserved for such purposes. My brother stood by as

I was injected with lysergic acid diethylamide – LSD to most people – and then imprisoned in a cell much like this one. I received the same treatment, daily, for a long time. I don't know *how* long, but a long time.'

Joseph stopped. His face was white and his hands were trembling with the horror of that memory. Ben watched as Annie stretched out her arm and placed it consolingly on the old man's leg.

'LSD gives you hallucinations – hours and hours of hallucinations, many of them totally terrifying. When they set me free, I was a mess,' he told them quietly. 'I was not fit to cope in society, and it wasn't long before I was placed in an institution for the insane. I tried to tell them what had happened to me, but of course nobody believed me. And that had been Lucian's plan all along.' Joseph winced slightly. 'In those days, mental institutions were not what they are today. I should know – I've seen enough of them over the past fifty years.'

'Fifty years?' Annie said disbelievingly. 'Is that how long you've been in institutions?'

Joseph nodded. 'Yes,' he said simply.

'And the place with the rats,' Ben asked him gently. 'The place we've just been. That was where—'

'That was where they gave me the injections,' Joseph finished his sentence for him. 'And that was why I had to come back. For fifty years they've been telling me that my memories are the figments of a paranoid imagination. I had to see the place once more just to prove to myself that they weren't.'

Annie was still staring at the old man. 'Fifty years,' she repeated. 'Fifty years in institutions, and you're not even mad.'

Joseph blinked. Then he smiled. He turned his bloodshot eyes to look at Annie. He stared at her for a full thirty seconds, and she winced under the force of that terrible gaze. Finally the old man spoke in a cracked, hoarse whisper.

'Oh, I'm mad, young lady,' he said. 'If that's the word you want to use, I'm perfectly mad. The drugs did their work very, very well. I'm prone to frequent psychotic episodes. I always was, even as a child, but milder then, easier to pass off as eccentricity; Lucian's treatment had the effect he wanted it to. And now, you see, I am without my medication, which only makes things worse.'

Ben and Annie glanced nervously at each other.

'But,' Joseph said suddenly and with a certain amount of force that startled the two of them, 'just because I'm mad, it doesn't make me wrong.' And as he spoke, the full vigour of his belief shone in his face. It made him look wild.

Annie shuffled uncomfortably, but Ben had another question. 'Joseph,' he asked seriously, 'if you've been in an institution for fifty years, if you're still prone to psychosis, if you need medication to keep it under control, can I ask you one thing?'

'What?' the old man said flatly.

'Why did they let you out?'

Joseph raised an eyebrow, as though he was surprised that Ben should have asked such a question. 'Let me out?' he said. 'Oh, they didn't let me out.'

'Then how—?' But Ben knew what the old man would say almost before he said it.

'I escaped,' Joseph replied matter-of-factly.

And as if that were an end to the matter, he huddled himself up again and carried on staring ahead of him, as if Ben and Annie weren't even there.

Chapter Fourteen

Air Commodore James Macpherson walked briskly down London's Horseferry Road and abruptly turned the corner into Marsham Street. It was dark now, and he was silently cursing to himself. He should have been on the motorway by this time, driving back up to Macclesfield for twenty-four hours' well-deserved leave. He had been looking forward to seeing his wife for ages, and it was just a shame Annie was away for a couple of days with her cousin. He smiled briefly to himself. Little Annie had grown up so fast – who'd have thought that she was old enough now to take a holiday on her own. At least she was just bird-watching – something nice and sedate, something safe, not like the kind of things some teenagers got up to nowadays.

Anyway, if he could get this meeting over and done with, maybe it wasn't too late to make a move. He looked up ahead of him and saw the modern black and white building of the Home Office looming up ahead. It didn't fill him with much hope for an early getaway – meetings at the Home Office were seldom speedy.

Minutes later he was being ushered to a far corner of the building, where a prim secretary asked him to wait in the comfortable ante-room to the office of the man he was coming to see. His name was Richardson. He had the bearing of a military man, but Macpherson did not know where or with whom he had served; that sort of information was classified. All he knew was that what Richardson didn't know about security matters you could write on the back of a postage stamp, and although he was irritated at the prospect of having to meet him, he was intrigued as well.

It was difficult for Macpherson to sit with his characteristically straight back in the comfortable leather chair he had been given, and he was glad when Richardson's door clicked open and the man himself beckoned him in with a wordless nod.

'Air Commodore,' Richardson greeted him curtly once they were both inside.

'It's nice to see you again,' Macpherson replied blandly.

'Have a seat. There's something I'd like you to take a look at.' Macpherson sat opposite Richardson's large oak desk and was handed two pieces of paper. He studied them closely.

One of them contained a short paragraph of text in a language he didn't understand – Chinese, maybe, he thought to himself. He flicked to the second sheet, which was in English, presumably a translation.

I have to write quickly, because they will find me soon. A weapon codenamed Vortex is being developed in the UK. It has been commissioned by a Russian oligarch and bought for a great price by the government of my country, the Democratic People's Republic of Korea. Strikes are planned against London, Los Angeles, New York and Madrid, and the weapons detection systems of none of these countries will be sufficient to counteract it. All I know is that the weapon is being developed covertly at a UK air force base without the knowledge of the authorities, and that its delivery is imminent. This must not happen. I cannot write more. They are coming for me. It is in your hands now.

The air commodore read it through several times, then looked up enquiringly at Richardson.

'North Korean origin,' the Home Office man said shortly. 'It came through earlier today.'

'Authentic?'

'That's what we're trying to determine. There's been

a certain amount of intelligence chatter – satellite intercepts and the like – about the word "vortex", which is why this was brought to my attention so quickly. But a lot of things don't make sense.'

'Such as?'

Richardson stood up. 'You are aware that this discussion falls under the constraints of the Official Secrets Act?'

'Of course.'

'Good. All right then. Only a small percentage of North Koreans have access to the Internet. Those who do are closely monitored. It is unlikely that anyone would be able to get a message like this through to the Ministry of Defence servers unless they were *extremely* technically adept.'

'You're saying it's a hoax?'

'I'm not saying anything yet. It certainly *came* from North Korea; but we know for sure that there are certain factions in their government who do not like the recent nuclear step-down that the Koreans are hinting at. This looks to me like a fairly standard piece of misinformation.'

'By some kind of breakaway group that wants to see North Korea as a major nuclear power?'

'Exactly.'

Macpherson looked back at the message. From his limited experience, he certainly couldn't say that it resembled the usual scraps of intelligence that came the way of the security services. Richardson was right: it was too obvious, as though someone were trying to fool them. He put the pieces of paper back down on Richardson's desk. 'I'm sure there's a reason you wanted to see me in particular about this.'

'Indeed,' Richardson replied. 'I want to know your opinion about the suggestion that this so-called weapon is being covertly developed at an RAF base.'

Macpherson thought carefully before answering. He considered the implications of what was being said: that at an RAF base somewhere in Britain, a high-level, top-secret weapon was being developed without the knowledge or authority of those in command; that there was some kind of renegade, covert operation in place. There were plenty of military research projects going on, of that there was no doubt. But they were controlled, overseen and documented. The idea that something of this magnitude could be going on without people like himself being in the know was, well, unthinkable.

He cleared his voice before he spoke. 'If you're asking my professional opinion,' he said clearly, 'I'd have to tell you that I think the idea is preposterous.'

Richardson nodded with satisfaction. 'Thank you, Air Commodore. I appreciate your frankness. I see no reason to suggest to the Home Secretary that we up the state of alert unless we receive any further evidence to corroborate what is being suggested here.'

'You'll let me know before that happens?' the air commodore asked.

'Of course,' Richardson replied. He stood up and offered Macpherson his hand, which was duly shaken. 'Thanks for your time. Family OK?'

'Fine, thank you,' Macpherson replied with a gentle smile.

'That daughter of yours, er . . .'

'Annie.'

'Of course, she must be, what . . .'

'Thirteen.'

'She's well?'

'Very well, thank you. Looking forward to joining the RAF herself one day. Now if you'll excuse me . . .'

'Of course,' Richardson said. 'Thanks again.'

Macpherson turned, walked out of the room, and left the building as quickly as possible. He couldn't wait to get home.

Ben and Annie stared at the old man in horror. His words seemed to echo round the concrete cell. *I escaped.*

'I know what you're thinking,' Joseph said, his voice unnaturally calm and level. 'You're thinking, how did we end up locked in a room with a paranoid psychotic who's just escaped from a mental institution?'

Ben bit his lip. 'No offence or anything, Joseph,' he said in a slightly strangled voice, 'but I was sort of thinking that, yes.'

'Of course you were,' the old man replied. 'You're a bright lad. But you don't need to worry, not about me – at least, not at the moment.'

Ben's eyes flicked towards Annie and then back to the old man. 'What do you mean, not at the moment?' he asked.

'Psychotic episodes,' Joseph replied distractedly. 'They come and go. At the moment, my mind is clear.'

One of Ben's eyebrows shot up. 'At the moment? What's that supposed to mean?'

'I hear voices,' he said. 'Not all the time, but more and more of late. Sometimes a shock – much like the one I have just experienced – will force them to recede. But without my medication, I know they will return. They tell me to do things, and sometimes I cannot distinguish between what is real and what is not.'

The old man's startling honesty silenced Ben.

'If I were you, however,' Joseph continued, 'I would not concern yourself unduly with my state of mind. I would ask yourself a different question. Like, why have we just been blindfolded, handcuffed and locked up.'

'Because we were following you,' Annie said hotly.

'Indeed. You followed me into Spadeadam, which

was the one thing I advised you not to do. Tell me, young lady, how old are you?'

'Thirteen,' Annie replied bullishly.

'And you, Ben?'

'Thirteen too.'

'I see,' Joseph continued. 'I myself am in my seventies. You'll understand, I hope, that I seem to have lost track of my precise age. I stopped celebrating birth-days a long time ago.'

'What's your point, Joseph?' Ben asked. He was beginning to get a bit tired of the old man's constantly cryptic comments – it was like being stuck in a cell with a teacher who knew the answer but refused to give it to them.

'Two young teenagers and a seventy-something,' Joseph answered. 'Not a huge threat to a troop of RAF soldiers, I'd have thought. Do you think the way we've been treated over the past couple of hours is how ordinary members of the RAF would be likely to treat us.'

'No,' Annie said immediately. 'They're well out of order, and when I tell—'

'Forgive me, my dear,' Joseph interrupted, 'but unless I'm very mistaken, you won't be telling anyone about what's happened. Not, at least, until it's too late.'

'You know what's going on, don't you, Joseph?' Ben asked suspiciously.

'Not really,' the old man replied. 'But I can make a few intelligent guesses.'

'Like what?'

Slowly, like an old deer rising precariously to his feet, Joseph stood up. The cut on his face looked swollen and sore. He wandered towards the metal doors of the cell and started absent-mindedly fiddling with the steel plate on the wall. 'Does it not strike you as odd,' he asked in that infuriatingly measured way, 'that my brother should still be here, in the same place where he was fifty years ago?'

Annie and Ben looked at each other and shrugged. 'I suppose,' Annie replied.

'So we must ask ourselves why that is.' Joseph continued to scratch at the metal plate with his finger-nail. 'I think we can safely say that it is not on account of his love of rare birds, can we not?'

The three of them stood in silence for a moment. His brow furrowed, Ben tried to work out what Joseph's mind was edging towards. 'You said you and your brother were physicists,' he ventured after a while.

'Good,' murmured Joseph, once more giving Ben the feeling he was some kind of apprentice to this strange old man.

Ben turned to Annie. 'Electronic warfare. Isn't that what you said they got up to at this place?'

Annie nodded mutely.

'Well that's it, isn't it? He stayed at Spadeadam because it gave him the opportunity to be around the field of study that interested him so much.'

Joseph continued to pick at the metal plate. 'I think you're right, Ben. But there's more to it than that.'

'Like what?'

The old man turned round sharply, and then waved his arms around him. 'All this,' he said.

'A cell?' Annie asked.

'Not just the cell. The entire underground bunker. You see, Lucian was here fifty years ago. He knew about these bunkers when they were built for their' – his lip curled into an expression of distaste – 'scientific research projects. I feel confident that the existence of the place where we are now is not common knowledge, and the opportunity to be able to continue his research in secret would be extremely attractive to my brother.'

As Joseph spoke, Ben found himself barely believing what the old man was suggesting. But then he remembered something – something he had read on the Internet back at the youth hostel. Hadn't he learned that excavations for a secret underground missile silo had been found at Spadeadam only a few years ago? There had been no plans or documents on record – officially the silo didn't even exist.

'Are you trying to tell me,' he asked slowly, 'that your brother has renegade RAF soldiers under his control, and that he's keeping us prisoner in an underground bunker which nobody knows exists while he continues his scientific research?'

'And he thinks we know what he's up to?' Annie added. 'This Vortex thing, whatever it is, he thinks we know what it is and that we're here to stop him?'

'But what *is* Vortex?' Ben asked in frustration.

'I don't know,' Joseph replied quietly. 'But I think we ought to find out, don't you?'

He looked piercingly at Ben, then Annie, then back to Ben again. As he did so, Ben struggled hard to decide what was the right thing to do. This man had just told him he heard voices that didn't exist. Should he believe him? Should he be talked into some fool's errand, to try and outwit these men who, if Joseph was right, were ruthless and dangerous? He stared hard at the old man, trying to find the madness in his eyes that had been so evident when they had been bombarded on the practice range.

Joseph stared back. His eyes seemed bright. Vivid. Determined. But they did not seem mad. Not at that moment, at least.

Ben took a deep breath. 'What are we going to do?' he asked.

A look of relief fell over Joseph's face. 'Thank you, Ben,' he said quietly. Then he turned to Annie. 'Are we all agreed that we need to try and get out of here?'

'Of course,' Annie replied. 'But how?'

Joseph turned back towards the metal plate on the wall. 'Do either of you have a key, or a coin – something to give us a bit of leverage?'

Ben grinned. 'I've got something even better than that,' he said with a certain amount of satisfaction. He reached down into his sock and pulled out his penknife. 'They took everything else, but they didn't take this. The pliers are a bit broken,' he apologized, 'but there's a good blade on it.'

Joseph took the penknife and unfolded the largest blade. He nodded with satisfaction, then turned back to the metal plate and forced the knife into the groove surrounding it. For a minute or two he worked away at the plate, while Ben and Annie stood there, holding their breath and listening to the scraping sound of the knife worrying against the metal echo around the cell. Just as Ben thought that the old man was not going to be successful, he saw him lever the plate away from the wall, to reveal a mass of wires behind.

'I thought so,' he muttered to himself as Ben and Annie drew closer.

'What is it?' Annie whispered.

'The wiring for the electric door,' Joseph stated. He peered at the tangle of colour-coded wires.

'Can you rewire it?' Ben asked tensely.

'Patience, Ben,' Joseph instructed, and continued to examine the wiring.

Ben and Annie waited in silence, a sudden nervousness having descended upon the room.

Finally Joseph spoke. 'I think it should be straightforward to open the doors,' he said confidently.

Ben licked his lips, which had become suddenly dry. 'OK,' he said, feeling as if he was improvising on the spot. 'Will you be able to close them again?'

'Yes,' Joseph replied. 'I think so.'

'Good. There might be a guard out there. He won't be expecting the doors to open, so when they do we'll have the element of surprise. Joseph, you'll be busy with the wiring, so it's going to be up to me and Annie to charge him. We'll need to get him back into the cell and close the doors before he can raise the alarm.'

'We're not going to have much time,' Annie said. 'Remember, these guys are armed.'

'I know,' Ben said solemnly. 'We have to move quickly.' He looked at Annie and Joseph in turn. 'Are you ready?' he asked.

Annie nodded.

'Joseph?'

'Wait,' he said. 'When I close the doors, I'll still be inside here. I'll do my best to jump out in time, but if I don't manage it, you two will have to go it alone.'

A chill crept over Ben's skin. 'If there's a guard

outside, you can't risk being stuck in here with him. If nothing else, he'll force you to open the doors again.'

Joseph shook his head. 'He can force me all he likes. If I rip the wiring out, the mechanism will be destroyed anyway. They'll have to yank the doors open from outside to get to us.' He gave a sardonic smile. 'And besides,' he said, 'I'm quite used to being locked up in cells. I'll almost be glad of the company.'

Ben breathed out heavily and shut his eyes. 'All right,' he said finally. 'But *try* and get out, OK.'

'Of course,' Joseph replied calmly.

'After three, then. One, two, three – *go!*'

As Ben spoke the word, Joseph pulled out two wires and touched them together. There was a spark at his fingertips, and the metal doors hissed slowly open. As Ben had predicted, they revealed a guard in RAF fatigues. He had clearly had his back to the door, but had reacted to the noise and turned round. Ben registered two things: the surprise on his face, and the fact that this was one of the same soldiers who had picked them up. 'Now!' he shouted to Annie, and the two of them lunged forward, pushing him heavily against the far wall. The soldier grunted as Annie placed a well-aimed blow in his stomach; winded, he bent double and Ben pulled his firearm from the holster by his side. He pressed the barrel of the gun against the soldier's back and pushed him forward. 'Get in the cell,' he instructed.

Still gasping for air, the soldier did as he was told, stumbling heavily through the open doors.

'Sit down in the corner and put your hands on your head,' Ben said, then he watched with satisfaction as the soldier followed his instructions to the letter. He looked over at Joseph. 'OK,' he said. 'Shut the doors.'

Joseph nodded, and as Ben stepped backwards out into the corridor he flicked two more wires together. The doors started to shut. 'Get out, Joseph!' Annie urged as the old man hurled himself towards them. There was an awful grinding as the heavy doors closed against the old man's body, but at the last moment he managed to slip through, Annie pulling at him with all her might. The doors closed firmly shut, leaving the soldier locked up inside.

'Will he be able to open the doors using the wires?' Ben asked tersely.

'Not probable,' he said. 'But just to be sure—' He looked meaningfully at the gun Ben held in his hand, and then at the keypad to the left of the doors. Ben understood what he meant. He flicked the small safety catch on the handgun, then aimed it at the keypad.

Bang!

The keypad exploded as the bullet hit it. The sound of the gun, however, seemed to reverberate along the corridor with a deafening echo. The trio looked at each other nervously. 'We'd better hope nobody heard that,' Annie muttered.

Ben nodded, not wanting to think of what would happen if their captors ran in this direction to find out what had happened. He looked down the corridor to his right. 'I think we came this way,' he said. 'Are we all agreed?'

Joseph and Annie nodded.

'Come on, then,' he instructed and, grasping his gun tightly, Ben led the way.

They walked briskly but quietly, desperately trying to remember the way back to the room in which Lucian had interrogated them. Each time they came to a corner, they flattened themselves against the wall while Ben peered round, gun at the ready, to check it was safe. Now and then, they would pass a door. When that happened, Ben would press his ear against it to see if there was any sound of voices; when he was sure it was silent, he would open the door, gun firmly at the ready, and check out what was inside.

Most of the rooms were empty. Others, however, clearly acted as store cupboards. There were shelves full of electronic equipment that meant nothing to Ben, as well as scientific implements, wires, batteries and even, in one room, boxes of plastic explosive. But there was no sign of any people. After several minutes of searching, it became clear that the dimly lit, maze-like concrete corridors of this underground warren were practically deserted; it also became clear that they were lost.

'How on earth are we supposed to find our way out of here?' Annie burst out suddenly.

Ben turned to see tears in her eyes. He gave Joseph a long look. 'I don't know,' he said quietly. 'I guess we just have to keep trying—'

He cut himself short. From somewhere – he wasn't sure where – he heard the sound of footsteps. The trio threw each other anxious glances, then pressed themselves hard against the wall. The footsteps grew louder, and they seemed to be coming along a corridor that ran at right angles to the one in which they stood. Ben gestured at the other two to run back out of sight, and the three of them scuttled down the corridor as quietly as they could, turning a corner just in time – Ben peered back to see two men continuing on their way. Although he was watching from a distance, he was sure that one of them was Flight Lieutenant Johnson.

As soon as they were out of sight, the trio followed. When they got to the end of the corridor, Ben peered round again in time to see them knock on a door, wait, and then walk inside.

'What should we do?' Annie whispered hoarsely.

'That was Johnson,' Ben replied. He turned to Joseph. 'I think we need to hear what they're saying, don't you?'

Joseph nodded and, feeling his blood beating through his veins, Ben led them towards the door.

It was dark at that end of the corridor, but Ben was glad of the darkness as they took up positions outside the partially open door and strained their ears to hear what was going on inside. A voice was speaking: Ben instantly recognized it as being Lucian's.

'There was really no need for you to come,' he said tersely. 'Everything is under control, and your presence here is a risk.'

A man with a thick Russian accent answered. 'My employer believes it is a risk worth taking,' he said darkly. 'If you are not satisfied with my presence, I suggest you consult with him.'

'No,' Lucian replied after a moment's thought. 'That won't be necessary.'

'Good,' the Russian replied emphatically.

A brief silence.

'I must say,' Lucian observed, 'that I'm surprised the North Koreans have bought it. I'd have thought the Iranians would have been drooling at the mouth.'

'You need not concern yourself with that,' the Russian replied insultingly. 'You and your men have been well paid to develop the project. My advice to you would be to concentrate on getting out of the country as soon as you can after Vortex is delivered.'

'Ah,' Lucian replied lightly, 'I'm glad you mentioned that. You have our fake passports?'

'They are all prepared. I will deliver them to you

when the time is right, along with your money. In the meantime, you will explain to me how this device works.'

There was a brief pause, and then Ben heard a low chuckle coming from Lucian. 'I see,' he said softly. 'Your beloved employer trusts you so much, he hasn't even told you what Vortex does.'

The Russian did not respond.

'Don't worry,' Lucian replied. 'Vortex is my baby. All proud parents like to show off their children, don't they?'

Ben strained his ears even more. He did not want to miss a single bit of the explanation that followed.

Lucian cleared his throat, as though he was about to address a public meeting. 'Any electronic device that works wirelessly – mobile phones, radio, wireless Internet connections – uses electromagnetic signals. Vortex is designed to interfere with these signals. The user simply decides which portion of the electro-magnetic spectrum is to be scrambled, and the area over which the effect is to take place, up to a maximum radius of fifteen miles.'

'It sounds very simple,' the Russian replied.

'So do most things, to the unscientific mind, my friend. In reality, of course, I have been working on this for more than five years. It is the only weapon of its kind in the world.'

As Lucian spoke, Ben became aware of Joseph. His face was red, and he had started muttering under his breath. 'Idiots!' he spat. 'Don't they realize what they could do? *Idiots!*'

'Be quiet, Joseph,' Ben whispered, but it was no good. The old man continued to curse and splutter.

'They're going to hear him, Ben,' Annie urged.

'I know,' Ben replied. 'Come on, let's get back round the corner.' Each of them grabbed one of Joseph's arms and pulled him back down the corridor and out of sight.

Joseph was still cursing. 'Those fools,' he raged. 'Don't they understand the implications? It all makes sense now. Lucian must have been working here helping the military with their electronic warfare tactics. But all the while, he's been secretly developing the technology for his own kind of war.'

'Er, Joseph,' Ben ventured. 'To be honest, it sounded to me like they're planning to switch off everyone's mobile phones. I've got to tell you that it really doesn't sound all that bad to me.'

Joseph took a deep breath, turned and stared directly at Ben. His face was alarming: sharp and serious, and it made Ben regret his brief moment of sarcasm.

'It may not sound that bad to you, young man, but let me be quite clear: disabling the electromagnetic spectrum over that kind of range would be disastrous.

It won't just be teenagers chatting on their telephones who will be affected.'

'Why?' Ben asked. 'What would happen?'

'You would probably know better than me, young man. Fifty years ago this technology was in its infancy; now it's commonplace, but I have only been able to read about it in scientific journals, and watch its effects on the television. You may not be able to *see* the electromagnetic spectrum, Ben, but you use it every day when you switch on the TV or listen to the radio. But that's not what an electromagnetic scrambler would target.'

'What, then?'

Joseph's face hardened. 'Think of sick people,' he said. 'Sick children. Patients who need X-rays and radiotherapy. Children with cancer. Activate Vortex, and all the technology which allows them to be treated would be rendered instantly useless. No TV to disseminate important news. No traffic lights on the streets. No Internet. One of these devices in every city would lead to an epidemic of suffering like we have not known for hundreds of years.'

Ben and Annie stared at him in shock.

'That's not all,' Joseph continued. 'The moment you switch such a device on, aircraft would not be able to communicate with air traffic control, or each other; their navigation systems would be rendered useless;

they would crash and burn. Hundreds of people could die. Maybe thousands. The emergency services would be completely ineffectual, unable to help anybody in the wake of such a disaster because they would not be able to communicate with each other. Whole cities could be plunged into chaos. It would be an unspeakable disaster; it would be a . . .' He seemed to struggle to find the words.

'It would be a Code Red situation,' Ben murmured to himself.

'As if that were not bad enough,' Joseph continued relentlessly, clearly not having heard what Ben had said, 'imagine the effect it could have on our defence systems. Position several of these devices correctly, and all our satellite warning systems would be instantly disabled: we would have no idea that we were under attack, and we would be in no position to order a counter attack. If somebody were to scramble the electromagnetic field correctly as a prelude to a nuclear attack, they could obliterate their enemy without any fear that their missiles could be destroyed. Believe you me, Ben Tracey, if that device works and falls into the wrong hands, it could spell disaster for millions of people across the world.'

A heavy silence fell as the impact of Joseph's words sank in.

Ben turned to Annie. 'I came away for a quiet

weekend of bird-watching,' he said almost accusingly. 'Instead, I find myself in the middle of another—' He looked down at the floor in disgust. 'I'm getting sick of this,' he muttered.

'Listen to me, you two,' Joseph was saying sharply. 'What my brother is doing *cannot* be allowed to happen.'

'But what can we do to stop it, Joseph?' Annie asked in desperation. 'You said it yourself – two teenagers and a seventy-something. What can we *do*?'

The question hung in the air as they stood there in that gloomy concrete corridor.

It was Joseph who spoke first. '*I* have to do something,' he stated, almost matter-of-factly. 'Lucian is my brother, and I must take responsibility for his actions.'

And with that, before either of them could do anything about it, he strode round the corner and back down the corridor. Annie gasped and Ben watched, stunned, as he approached the partially open door. Joseph turned back to them, gave them a sad little smile of comradeship and then pushed the door wide open.

'This is not what science is for, Lucian,' he said in a clear, ringing voice. 'This is not what science is for, and it has to stop. Now.'

Chapter Fifteen

'Who is this?'

In the silence that followed Joseph's shock entrance into the room, Ben and Annie had tiptoed back up to the door. The Russian man was speaking, and he sounded as though he was getting increasingly angry.

'I said, who is this?'

'Are you going to tell him, Lucian, or am I?'

A pause.

'It's nobody important,' Lucian hissed. 'You don't need to worry about it.'

'I beg to differ—' Joseph's voice rang clearly; but it was interrupted by a sudden thud, and then a groan. Instinctively, Ben made as if to burst into the room and help the old man, who had clearly just been dealt a debilitating blow, but Annie forcefully held him back.

'Not yet,' she hissed, as voices started up again in the room.

'Don't tell me what I do and don't need to worry about,' the Russian snapped. 'I do not need to tell you what would happen if people found out about this – you for one do not strike me as the type of man who would do well in a prison cell for the rest of your life.'

'That won't happen,' Lucian countered. 'I can deal with this person.'

'You will deal with him in the way I see fit. My employer is quite clear on this matter. If anybody else becomes aware of the existence of this weapon, they are to be eliminated immediately.'

'Eliminated?' Lucian's voice sounded scornful. 'Don't be ridiculous. This isn't Chechnya, my friend. We can't just go around killing people whenever we feel like it. I will deal with this . . . I'll deal with him, OK?'

'No,' the Russian stated flatly. 'It is not OK. I want him dead before Vortex leaves this place. Your money depends on it, do you understand?'

There was the sound of a fist banging on a hard surface. 'I've told you already, I've been working on this for years. If you think you can start messing me about with the money now—'

Lucian was interrupted by a weak voice. 'Think of what you're saying,' Joseph gasped.

'SHUT THAT LUNATIC UP!' Lucian screamed,

and once more there was the sound of scuffling. Ben winced as he heard the unmistakable sound of someone being brutally punched and then falling heavily to the floor.

'It seems to me,' the Russian almost purred, 'that you are a very long way from being able to deal with this intruder. I want him dead before the weapon leaves here, do you understand?'

Lucian sniffed. 'I understand,' he said, seemingly through gritted teeth.

'Then that concludes our business for now. Let me know when it is done.'

Ben and Annie heard movement in the room, and in an instant they realized that the Russian was about to walk out. Quickly they turned and ran, sprinting down the corridor as deftly as their feet would carry them; adrenaline burned in Ben's veins as he prayed that the strange owner of that harsh Russian voice would not see them slip round the corner, and as they hid in the shadows, he half expected to be at the wrong end of a gun at any minute. Nervously he fingered the firearm that he had taken from the guard outside the cell; other than that, they kept perfectly still, their breath held, as they listened to the sound of footsteps dying away.

Only when all was quiet did Annie speak. 'What are we going to do?' she whispered.

Ben's brow furrowed as he tried to think his way

through all this. To all intents and purposes, they were stuck down here. They didn't know their way around, and he was pretty sure that as soon as anyone came across them, they'd be history. Moreover, it was only a matter of time before someone discovered that the guard they had incarcerated in their cell was missing. When that happened, all hell would break loose.

Annie interrupted his thoughts. 'Lucian wouldn't really do that, would he?' she trembled. 'Kill him, I mean. His own brother.'

'I don't know,' Ben replied grimly. 'If what Joseph told us was true – and I don't really see any reason to doubt him – then that brother of his is a pretty nasty piece of work. Look what he did to him all those years ago.'

Annie looked troubled. 'But he didn't kill him. Surely that's something, isn't it?'

Ben wanted to agree with her, but he couldn't. 'I don't think we can count on the kindness of Joseph's brother to get us out of this, do you?'

Annie thought for a moment, then shook her head. 'No,' she said finally. 'I don't.'

Silently, Ben held up his handgun. 'I don't know about you,' he said, 'but it seems to me that this is the only ace we're holding.'

His cousin's eyes narrowed. 'Listen to me carefully, Ben,' she said. 'Flight Lieutenant Johnson is still in that room. He's RAF, you can bet your bottom dollar that he's armed, and he's been highly trained. If you rush in there all guns blazing, I promise you he'll have a bullet in your head before you can raise an arm.'

The warning hung there in the air between them. Eventually Ben nodded his head. 'You're right,' he said. 'But if we walk in there unarmed, we'll just be taken prisoner again, and who knows what they'll do with us this time—'

'Quiet!' Annie hushed him. 'Footsteps!'

Ben listened. Sure enough, he heard the unmistakable sound of people leaving the room. And then a voice, so loud that it made them both jump. 'How dare you!' they heard Joseph almost shout. 'How dare you treat me like this and leave my brother alone there with that wicked device!'

A thump.

A pained cough.

'Shut up,' they heard Johnson growl.

Annie's eyes went steely. 'Let's follow them,' she whispered with determination in her voice.

'No,' Ben replied forcefully. 'Don't you see? Joseph was just letting us know that Lucian's alone with the device. He's in charge round here. If we can get him to do what we say, that makes us in charge. You said it yourself – we'd be stupid to go face to face with Johnson.'

184

'But Joseph—' Annie started to say, and Ben wondered if he saw the beginnings of tears in her eyes.

'I know,' he whispered. 'I know. But this is the best chance we have of saving him – and stopping Vortex from seeing the light of day.'

Annie bit her lip. 'Do you think it's as bad as Joseph said?' she asked.

Ben breathed out heavily. 'I don't know,' he replied. 'But I don't think it's a risk we can afford to take, do you?'

Annie shook her head.

'OK then,' Ben said tersely. 'Let's go.' And with the gun firmly in his grip, he moved stealthily back up the corridor, round the corner and towards the door. It was shut now, and the two of them waited outside for a brief moment as they prepared themselves for what was to follow. Then Ben stretched his gun arm out straight, pointing the firearm in front of him, and slowly, quietly opened the door.

Lucian was there, but he did not see them at first. His back was turned, and he stooped over a desk against the far wall, resting his hands on the table and seeming to stare into space. His back was hunched, and the hair on the back of his head thin: from this angle, he looked to Ben like a very old man. An old man who was carrying a tremendous weight on his shoulders.

In front of him, in the middle of the room, was

another table, a large one, with extremely bright halogen lights beaming down onto it from the ceiling. And on the table, gleaming in the bright light, was a metallic cylinder. It was about the size of a small suitcase, and there was something rather elegant about the smooth, polished metal and the surprisingly few controls and displays that were embedded along the top of the cylinder.

Ben found himself momentarily transfixed. That was it, he told himself. That was Vortex. It had to be.

It was a beautiful object. Slick and shiny. But it was capable of so much terror.

He dragged his eyes from the device and looked back at Lucian. He noticed that his gun hand was trembling slightly, so he did his best to steady it, then spoke in as firm a voice as he could muster. 'Turn round slowly, Lucian, and put your hands on your head.'

Lucian didn't move.

'I said, turn round!' Ben instructed more firmly. 'Now!'

With infinite slowness, Lucian's body creaked to its full height like a snake rising from the ground. He refused to put his hands on his head, instead looking at Ben and Annie over his round glasses with an expression half of amusement, half of dislike.

'Your hand is shaking, boy,' he whispered.

Ben cursed himself inwardly for allowing his nerves to show, but he did not let his aim waver.

'Put your hands on your head,' he repeated. 'I mean it, Lucian. I'm not messing around.'

Lucian's lined face moulded itself into a sneer. 'How old are you, boy?' he practically whispered.

'That doesn't matter. Put your hands on your head.'

'Oh, I don't think I'll be doing that. I can tell a bluff when I see one. I know perfectly well that you don't have the faintest idea how that gun works. Put it down before you hurt yourself.' He took a confident step towards them.

Ben narrowed his eyes. The old man in front of him had a look of such supreme arrogance it was all he could do to suppress his anger. Their eyes locked, and Ben stared at him emotionlessly before it became clear what he had to do to get Lucian's attention.

The old man took another step forward. 'Ben . . .' Annie breathed urgently.

Ben didn't reply. Slowly he lowered his arm so that the gun was pointing towards the floor. Lucian smiled unpleasantly. 'Good boy,' he said, as though he were talking to an obedient dog.

But before he could take another step towards the two of them, Ben raised the gun again. This time he was not pointing it at Lucian; he was pointing it at the metal canister on the table between them. 'Let's see if I can't guess how this gun works, shall we?' he said with a half-smile.

And with a squeeze of the trigger, he fired.

Almost instantaneously, there were two noises: the loud crack of the gun, and a more tinny ring as the bullet ricocheted off the metal device, leaving a small dent in the sturdy metal exterior. Annie stifled a scream as the bullet whistled past them to embed itself in the wall. Lucian's reaction could not have been more extreme. The lazy arrogance fell from his face and he stepped forward towards the device, almost caressing it. 'What do you think you're playing at?' he demanded, aghast. 'Do you have any idea what you could have done?'

'Yeah,' Ben replied. 'Actually, I do.' He aimed the gun back in Lucian's direction. 'Now put your hands on your head like I told you. We're going to have a little chat.'

'What could *we* possibly have to chat about?' Lucian spat. All the colour had drained from his face the moment Ben had shot at the device on the table, and although he still sounded contemptuous and superior, he looked like half the man he had when they had first walked in.

'Joseph, for a start. Where have they taken him?'

'It's no concern of yours, boy.'

Ben aimed the gun back at the device.

'No!' Lucian shouted. 'Stop. Wait.'

Ben raised an eyebrow. 'You'd better start talking,' he said, 'because I *will* shoot again.'

'OK, OK,' Lucian stuttered. 'He's being escorted off the premises.'

Immediately, Ben fired another shot at the device. This time it caused an even bigger dent towards the centre and, once again, the ricocheting bullet shot into the wall – on the other side of the room this time. 'Don't lie to me, Lucian,' he said. 'I overheard that Russian man telling you to kill him, and I don't believe for a minute that you'd just let him go, not after everything you've done to keep us out of the way.'

Lucian's eyes narrowed. For some reason he glanced up to the ceiling, but then he stared back at Ben and moistened his lips with his tongue before speaking again. 'Very well,' he whispered. 'If you think you're old enough to ask the question, then you'd better be prepared to hear the answer. My idiot brother is being taken to a target range, much like the one where you were discovered snooping around. There is a training exercise at dawn. The principal target there is a newly constructed hut. Joseph is being locked in there, and it will definitely be destroyed during the training exercise.'

'You're sick,' Annie declared.

'I'm not sick, missie,' he retorted with sudden anger. 'I'm a pragmatist.'

'You're a nutter, more like,' she replied. 'What's with all this James Bond stuff? Why didn't you just shoot him while you had the chance?'

'I wouldn't expect you to understand, little girl,' he said as insultingly as he could.

'Oh, we understand all right,' Ben said quietly. 'You're doing it this way because you don't want his blood on your hands. If he's killed during a training exercise, everyone will think it's just a terrible accident caused as a result of him nosing around in a place where he shouldn't be.'

Lucian smiled again. 'Very good,' he whispered.

'How could you do that to him?' Ben asked in shock. 'He's your brother. First you put him in a mental asylum all his life, now this.'

'Ah.' Lucian's eyes widened. 'Is that what he told you?' He turned round and walked away from them back towards the wall, before spinning back to look at them angrily. 'Well let *me* tell you,' he said waspishly, 'that my brother was heading for a life in and out of mental institutions from before he was even your age.'

'We've seen the room where you did it, Lucian,' Ben countered. 'We've seen the place where you made your brother's mental instability ten times worse.'

'He was going to blow the whistle!' Lucian shouted. 'He was going to ruin important research.'

'Some things are more important than research,' Ben told him.

'Don't be so naïve. People had tried to put a stop to our experiments before dear Joseph had the idea. Every single one of them disappeared. I was doing Joseph a favour, stopping the authorities from killing him. He should be thanking me, but he's too crazy to know any different.'

'Funny, isn't it,' Annie observed as though to herself, 'that after fifty years in psychiatric hospitals, he doesn't quite see it that way. And you know another thing that's funny? That for all this talk of what a big favour you did him, you're happy to let him die now.'

Annie's barbed comment seemed to echo all around the room.

'He knew what he was doing, interfering with my work once again,' Lucian told her.

'I thought you said he was crazy. If he's crazy, surely he *doesn't* know what he's doing.'

'It hardly matters,' Lucian spat. He pointed at the metal cylinder. 'Some things are more important. Do you have any idea how many lives my invention could save?'

'*What?*' Ben and Annie said in unison.

'Of course!' Lucian hollered, waving his arms slightly maniacally in the air. 'If the North Koreans – or whoever – get their hands on it, it will stop them from resorting to nuclear weapons. They won't *need* to go nuclear, because they'll have a far more effective weapon at their disposal.' As he spoke, his eyes betrayed the light of a zealot.

'Really?' Ben asked, his voice trembling though he did his best to keep it level. 'Well, try telling that to the people who'll die when their planes fall out of the sky as a result of your toy.'

Lucian shrugged. 'Collateral damage,' he stated. 'In every conflict there has to be a certain amount of acceptable loss. If you think it doesn't happen with our current systems of warfare, then you really are more stupid than I thought.'

But Ben just shook his head. 'You know what?' he said, not allowing his gun to waver from Lucian's direction. 'You're the crazy one, not your brother.'

Lucian snorted. 'It's amazing how many people seem to think so,' he said. 'Crazy old Lucian, stuck at Spadeadam for all his working life. Those do-gooding RAF muppets above ground treat me like I'm just as crazy as Joseph. But they're not the ones about to receive a five-million-pound payment and a one-way ticket to anywhere they want in the world. They're not the ones who have spent the past five years working on a project that governments around the world would pay millions to get their hands on.'

'Just shut up, Lucian!' Ben shouted him down, sickened by the man's greed. 'You're not going any-where until we've found Joseph and made sure he's—'

But before Ben could finish, something silenced him. From the ceiling of the room, he became aware of a dull red light, flashing metronomically. He glanced up at it, and was aware that Lucian was also looking at the light with satisfaction.

'It's flashing all the way down the corridor, Ben,' he heard Annie say tensely from behind him.

Lucian smiled his unpleasant smile once more. 'Of course it is,' he said. 'It's been so nice having this little chat with you – thank you for being so interested in what I have to say. And while we've been jabbering away, of course, Flight Lieutenant Johnson has been a good little soldier and checked your cell, just as I told him to. They've discovered you're missing, and they're taking the necessary precautions.'

Ben and Annie looked at each other with barely disguised panic.

'You might as well put the gun down,' Lucian continued implacably, 'and stop your silly, childish little games. This is grown-ups' business now. They're shutting the place down and there's no way out. And when they get their hands on you, you'll be taken to the same place as Lucian. Sorry, kids, but I'm afraid you're not in for a very good day.'

Chapter Sixteen

The red light continued to flash. Somehow Ben felt it would be less sinister if there had been some kind of siren to go with it, but there wasn't: just a repetitive, silent warning that they were in real danger. Each time it lit up, it bathed Lucian's face in its dusty red glow: the flatness in his eyes and the strange effect of the lighting made him look somehow demonic.

Ben's mind was a mass of confusion, but he had to think quickly. No doubt some of Lucian's renegade soldiers were already on their way, heavily armed and under strict instructions to apprehend them, and then who could say what? There was no point running – they would only get lost in this underground warren of dingy concrete corridors – and soon enough they would be found and overcome. 'What are we going to do, Ben?' he heard Annie whisper.

'The only thing we can,' he said tensely as a sketchy plan started to form in his head. It wasn't much, but it would have to do until he could think of something better. He took a step towards Lucian, still brandishing the handgun. 'You're going to get us out of here,' he instructed, 'and you're going to take us to Joseph.'

One of the old man's eyebrows shot up. 'Really?' he asked sarcastically. 'And why would I do that? What possible reason would I have when I know there are armed soldiers on their way to deal with you?'

Abruptly, Ben walked around the table bearing Vortex and rushed up to Lucian. 'You're going to do it because you know we haven't got a thing to lose. If it's a choice between being blown to smithereens with Joseph, or shooting you, I swear I'll do what I have to do.'

Ben struggled to keep control of his emotions. He didn't really think he would ever be able to bring himself to shoot a man, even someone as loathsome as Lucian, but he couldn't let on that this was the case. Their lives depended on it. It seemed to work. As he thrust the gun into the loose flesh of Lucian's neck, the old man appeared suddenly wrong-footed and scared. 'I *will* shoot you,' Ben whispered with all the seriousness he could muster. Then, without taking his eyes from his hostage's face, he spoke to his cousin. 'Annie, are you wearing a belt?'

'Yeah. Why?'

'Take it off. We need to tie his hands behind his back. Do it tightly.'

Immediately Annie was there, belt in hands. Lucian, his face full of hatred, obediently put his arms behind his back, then winced slightly as Annie pulled the leather straps firmly around his wrists before tying it into a tight and sturdy knot. 'He won't get out of that,' she said.

'Right.' Ben was improvising as he went along, but he knew he had to sound sure of himself. He moved behind Lucian, pointed the gun between his shoulder blades and dug it in sharply. He felt his hand shaking as he did so. He didn't like holding a gun. It didn't feel right. 'Walk,' he said with more confidence than he felt. 'You're going to take us to the exit. Mess up and I'll shoot.'

Lucian stood still. 'You'll never make it,' he said. 'They'll be on their way even now.'

'Shut up and walk,' Ben growled. Slowly, Lucian made his way to the door, Ben following, the gun still pressed against the old man's back and Annie by his side. They started to walk down the corridors, which Lucian navigated with ease. Ben was acutely aware of the fact that he couldn't be sure if his hostage was leading them in the correct direction or not; he just had to trust that he had instilled sufficient fear into the old man to stop him from trying it on. It was a long shot – Lucian hadn't reacted to being at the wrong end of the barrel of a gun in quite the way he had expected. In fact, he had seemed far more distressed at the idea of his metal cylinder being damaged than anything else.

He jabbed the gun sharply into Lucian's back. 'Faster,' he said, and the old man picked up pace.

It was eerie, hurrying along those deserted corridors with the red lights flashing silently. Every time they turned a corner, Ben expected to see a group of heavily armed soldiers waiting for them, guns at the ready; but they never appeared. 'How close are we to the exit?' Ben demanded when they had been walking for a couple of minutes.

'Too close.' A voice rang out clearly from behind them, and they came to an abrupt halt. Ben's blood turned to ice as he realized they had been so concerned with checking what was coming up ahead of them that they had forgotten to look over their shoulder.

'The girl's in my sights,' the voice informed them. 'I'm going to count to five. If you haven't put the gun on the ground by then, I'll shoot her.'

Ben's eyes flicked over to Annie. She had instinctively put her hands in the air.

'One.'

He desperately tried to think what to do.

'Two.'

He could try and spin Lucian round so they were both standing in front of Annie.

'Three.'

But he couldn't risk a sudden movement. These guys weren't messing around.

'Four.'

Think, Ben. *Think.*

'F—'

'All right!' he shouted. 'All right, I'm putting it down.' He closed his eyes, lowered his arm then turned round. The soldier who had caught them was standing about ten metres away. He had an assault rifle aimed directly at Annie's back, and his finger was poised over the trigger in readiness. His face was filled with un-disguised fury, and Ben realized instantly that this was the same guy they had locked in their cell.

'Put the gun down on the floor in front of you,' the soldier growled.

Ben did as he was told.

'Now kick it in my direction.'

He tapped the gun with his shoe and it slid a little way along the ground. The soldier approached, the butt of the gun still firmly dug into his shoulder as he aimed alter-nately at Annie and then Ben. Within seconds he was right up close to them. Lucian pushed past Ben and stood behind the soldier, a satisfied smirk on his face. 'About time for us to stop the heroics, wouldn't you say?'

The soldier grinned slightly at Lucian's comment, but he kept the rifle trained on Ben and Annie.

Lucian addressed the soldier. 'The exit, now. I'll go up front and you follow behind. There's a truck outside, and we haven't got much time. We need to be at the training ground before sunrise.' He turned back to the two cousins and gave them an unpleasant look. 'Playtime's over, kids,' he told them, before returning his gaze to his associate.

'If they try to run away,' he said, 'shoot them.'

Chapter Seventeen

At the exit, two soldiers stood guard. They took in what was happening in a single glance, and at a nod from Lucian one of them opened the doors. Beyond the doors was an old set of stone steps leading upwards. Ben and Annie followed Lucian up, hotly aware that they still had a gun pointed at them from behind.

Outside it was still dark, and as Lucian had predicted there was a truck waiting. Ben and Annie were hustled into the back seat, while the soldier took the wheel and Lucian sat in the passenger seat, twisting his body round so that he could point the gun at them.

They drove in silence. Ben dug his fingernails nervously into his palms, desperately trying to think of a way out of this, but he couldn't think straight with Lucian pointing a gun straight at him. The truck rumbled and juddered around the edge of a thick forest and so, more as a means of keeping calm than anything else, he concentrated on remembering the route they were taking. If they managed to escape – and it was a very big if – he knew they would have to return to the underground bunker and do something about Vortex.

Vortex. The very thought of it made him shiver. Joseph's description of what it could achieve rang in his head, and every time he closed his eyes he saw the horrifying image of patients lying in hospital beds, weak and wasting away, with anxious doctors by their side unable to do anything to help. He saw aeroplanes falling from the sky and crashing into populated buildings. He saw the fear in people's eyes as they watched bodies burn and die.

Could Joseph be right? Could this weapon be as disastrous as he said?

And then he remembered the look in Lucian's eyes when he boasted about the money he was being paid. Why would anyone give him millions of pounds to develop this weapon if it wasn't going to be horribly effective? Why would it be so top secret?

'It will kill thousands of people, you know,' he heard himself saying quietly.

Lucian didn't reply.

'Their blood will be on your hands. You do realize that, don't you?'

The old man snorted scornfully. 'I'm a lot older

than you,' he said. 'I understand things you don't.'

Ben looked at him scornfully. 'I bet there aren't many old men who would think that killing your own brother is a good thing to do.'

'Forgive me,' Lucian replied waspishly, 'but there aren't many old men who have my intellect. And if you think I'm going to let my lunatic brother – or you two, for that matter – get in the way of my creation, I'm afraid you are sadly mistaken.' His eyes flicked briefly out of the window. 'RAF Spadeadam,' he said almost thoughtfully. 'They have a motto. *Si vis pacem, para bellum*. Normally I don't find that military types have much to say of any interest, but in this instance, I have to make a grudging exception. I take it you do not understand what it means.'

Ben stared flatly at him, unwilling to admit that he was right. But just as the old man started to open his mouth again, Annie spoke.

'If you wish for peace,' she said clearly, 'prepare for war.'

Lucian looked at her in surprise. 'Very good,' he murmured.

'The thing is,' Annie replied with a confidence that surprised Ben, given their situation, 'that *you're* the one who's got it wrong. *You're* the one who doesn't under-stand it.'

'I hardly think so.'

'Of course you don't. Because you're blinded by your arrogance and your belief in your so-called intelligence.'

'Shut up,' Lucian replied.

'*Or what?*' Annie raged. 'You're going to shoot me? I hardly think so, if you're going to all this trouble to cover your tracks. So you might as well listen to me. Preparing for war is one thing; developing weapons that will harm innocent people – even children – is another. And if you reckon that giving Vortex to oppressive regimes is a sure-fire way to stop a nuclear war, then you're even more misguided than I thought. Our armies and our governments do a pretty good job of that without any unasked-for help from you. You think you're cleverer than everyone else, but you're not. You're arrogant and greedy, and even we can see that.'

By the time she had finished her tirade, Annie was almost breathless. Ben studied Lucian's face intently, fearfully looking for signs that his cousin might have pushed him over the edge. But there were none. He remained stony-faced, as if he hadn't even heard her accusations.

'Drive quicker,' he said blandly to the soldier next to him. 'We haven't got much time.'

The vehicle started to speed up, and as it did so, Ben became aware of the sickness of anticipation that was churning in his stomach.

It could have been five minutes later or it could have

been an hour – time suddenly seemed to have little meaning – when the truck started to slow down. Ben looked through the window and peered out into the darkness. He thought he could see huts in the distance, much like the ones that had been on the practice range the previous day, but as he squinted his eyes he could see that this was a much larger range. As the truck came to a halt, Lucian told them to get out; Ben and Annie did as they were told, and were instructed to walk across the field in amongst the huts and the rubble. There were other things there too: the blown-out carcasses of old cars, a tank like the one they had seen before. Ben couldn't concentrate on them too much, though – he was too acutely aware of the guns being pointed at them as Lucian and the soldier walked behind.

As they walked, the darkness oozed into the cold grey of dawn, and as if from nowhere Ben became aware of the dawn chorus filling the air with its deafening throng. When he had heard that sound only a couple of days before, it had filled him with excitement and wonder; now, though, it seemed ominous, as though it were foretelling something. Something bad.

Eventually they approached a hut in the middle of the practice range. It looked as though it had been newly built, and was constructed of rough, untreated timber – clearly this was not a structure that anyone expected to be there for a long time. On the door was a heavy metal padlock. 'You have the key?' Lucian asked the soldier.

He didn't reply; he simply stepped up to the hut, laid his rifle against the side and unlocked the padlock. 'Get in,' he growled.

Nervously, Ben and Annie walked through the door. It was dark inside, but by the weak light that spilled in, Ben could see Joseph there. He was sitting in the corner, trembling, his hair dishevelled and his face bruised. He didn't seem to register their arrival. Annie rushed towards him and touched her hand lightly to his beaten face; even then it was as if they weren't there.

Lucian spoke from the doorway. 'You seem to know something about the RAF, my girl,' he commented, 'so perhaps you would like some idea of what is about to happen. In about twenty minutes there will be a flyover by an A Ten Tankbuster aircraft. You've heard of the Tankbuster, I take it?'

'Yeah,' Annie stated. 'I've heard of it.'

'Good. They will be firing depleted uranium shells at around seventy rounds per second. As you probably know, such weapons can be' – he stopped, as though he were choosing his words carefully – 'reasonably destructive.' He looked over at Joseph, narrowing his eyes slightly, and then stepped backwards. 'Lock them in,' he told the soldier.

The door closed in front of him, and in the darkness they could hear the unmistakable sound of a key in the lock; moments later, the engine of the truck started up, and the vehicle drove away.

It was Ben who spoke first. 'Depleted uranium shells?' he asked. 'What are they?'

'You don't want to know.'

'Actually, I do.'

Annie sighed impatiently. 'Depleted uranium is a by-product of the nuclear power industry. It's very dense, which makes it an effective material for ammunition.'

'Right,' Ben replied, his voice a bit tight. 'And, er, seventy rounds per second. That's quite a lot, isn't it?'

'Yes, Ben. It's quite a lot. If we get hit by those things, chances are they won't even find our bodies.'

Ben took a deep, shaky breath; it was all he could do to stop his limbs from trembling. 'Then we'd better think of a way to get out of here. And fast.'

'I've already tried.' Joseph's voice came weakly from the corner of the hut. 'There's no way out. We're locked in.'

Surprised by the fact that he had suddenly spoken, Ben and Annie spun round to look at him. 'We can't give up now,' Ben stated. 'There must be a way out.' He approached the door and banged against it. It shuddered slightly in its frame. 'It's a cheaply built hut,' he said. He remembered how easily Annie had knocked down the posts on the perimeter fence. 'What do you think?' he asked her. 'Can we break through this wood?'

Annie joined him and she too banged on the door. Once more it rattled. 'I don't know,' she said. 'Maybe if we can pound it enough, but we might not have enough time.'

Ben shrugged. 'Got any better ideas?'

'Not really, no.'

'Then let's do it,' he said urgently. 'Come on, we need to work fast.'

They started to kick against the door, doing their best to aim at the same spot about halfway up each time. Annie's kicks seemed a lot more effective than Ben's – her tae kwon do training allowed her to put the full force of her body into it. For several minutes, they pounded away, their noisy kicks echoing regularly around the hut. The door seemed to rattle increasingly, but after several minutes of solid work, they did not seem to be any closer to breaking it down.

'This is useless,' Ben muttered angrily, wiping sweat from his brow. 'We've got to try harder. Those planes will be here any—'

And as he spoke, he heard them.

The three of them exchanged a nervous look. They all recognized the distant drone, of course. It was the sound of approaching aircraft, and it was getting louder. Without speaking, Ben and Annie resumed their desperate attempt to break the door down: the sound of the planes in the distance made them redouble their efforts.

It grew louder. And louder.

When the first round of shells fell, their reverberations knocked them both off their feet – for a minute, Ben thought it had been a direct hit, but when he realized that they were still in one piece, he pushed himself painfully to his feet to start kicking at the door again.

Annie, however, had beaten him to it. She was standing a couple of metres from the door, a look of intense concentration on her face as she raised her arms in a way that immediately reminded Ben of how she had looked when he had walked into her bedroom only a few days ago.

'Stand back,' she said under her breath.

A Tankbuster screamed overhead.

'This is our last chance, Annie,' Ben whispered. 'Make it a good one.'

'I'll do my best.' Another bomb blasted nearby.

She took a deep breath, closed her eyes, and launched herself at the door. With an enormous crack, the wood splintered down the middle.

Ben's eyes widened, and without waiting for any

instruction from Annie he started kicking down the splintered wood. It fell away from the door with surprising ease, and within seconds there was a gap through which they could all squeeze.

The two of them looked back at Joseph. He was staring around the hut, as though listening for something he couldn't hear, and he hadn't even seemed to notice that they had broken their way out, so they ran back to him and with all their strength pulled him to his feet, then dragged him towards the door and pushed him through the hole.

And for a split second they stood perfectly still, taking in the scenes of devastation around them.

It was like a war zone. The noise was deafening; clouds of thick dust surrounded them; planes scorched overhead, firing the depleted uranium shells in what seemed like a completely random way. As soon as they hit the earth they exploded into massive craters, or destroyed huts, blasting them into piles of rubble. Like rabbits in headlights, the three of them stood still, agog at the scenes of destruction. There were twice as many planes as last time, twice as many bombs – and there was nowhere to run and hide. They were in the middle of a huge area of grassland, and the forest they had skirted around was a long way distant.

'*What are we going to do?*' Annie screamed.

'*I don't know!*' shouted Ben. He looked desperately

around. Ammo was falling as far as he could see – it would take precious minutes they didn't have to run from the field of war and it would be like running into a hailstorm of deadly firepower . . .

And then his eyes fell upon the tank.

It was about thirty metres away, heavy and imposing; as far as Ben could tell it looked identical to the Chieftain Mark 10 Annie had pointed out yesterday. It was old and spattered in mud, but still looked awesome and threatening, the barrel of its enormous gun pointing belligerently out at a forty-five-degree angle. Maybe they could get some protection inside there, Ben thought to himself; who knows, it might even be operational.

Annie was looking at him, and seemed to know what he was thinking. 'Let's go for it!' she shouted. They each grabbed one of Joseph's arms and hustled him in the direction of the huge armoured vehicle. They were only metres away from the hut when a burst of shells fell directly on top of it, and the whole thing exploded, sending huge, ugly splinters of wood flying that missed them only by a miracle.

They ran even faster towards the tank.

'What are our chances of surviving a direct hit?' Ben yelled at Annie, his voice hoarse from trying to make himself heard above the sound of the planes.

'Not good,' she replied, 'with or without the tank.

But at least we'll be protected from shrapnel and flying debris if we get inside.'

'OK. How do we get in?'

'Up the top.'

Annie clambered onto the khaki chassis of the tank while Ben helped Joseph up the side before climbing up himself. His cousin lifted a metal disc hinged onto the turret, and the three of them dropped inside the tank, then closed the top behind them.

The interior of the Chieftain was like nothing Ben had ever seen – a metallic, industrial mess of displays, pedals and levers, wires and buttons. It was dingy – the only light coming through a small peephole in front of him that gave a limited amount of vision. A worn-out padded seat with holes in it was situated in the middle of the tank, in front of the controls, and Ben took his place there. As soon as he sat down, there was a massive explosion nearby: the whole tank seemed to shudder, and the three of them were knocked roughly against the metal walls. Annie cried out in pain, and Ben moved to see that she was OK; Joseph was already there, however; his eyes were suddenly alert again as he held her firm to stop her hurting herself as a result of a second explosion that rocked the tank once more.

'We're no safer in here than we were out there,' Joseph said. 'We need to get away.'

'Too right,' Ben said grimly. He looked at the jumble

of mechanical equipment in front of him. They meant nothing.

'There should be a starter button somewhere,' Annie said through clenched teeth.

Ben scoured the controls. Sure enough there was a large, brown button in front of him. He shrugged, took a deep breath, and hit it.

To Ben's total surprise, the noisy engine coughed and spluttered into life. Outside, there was another deafening explosion.

'Drive it!' Annie screamed. 'Get us out of here!'

'I don't know how!'

'The pedals,' she yelled at him. 'One's an accelerator, one's a brake. Steer left and right using those red levers on either side.'

Ben located everything she was talking about. Sure enough, on each side of his seat there was a lever, not unlike the handbrake of a car. He gripped them firmly, peered through the viewing window, and gingerly pressed his foot down on the accelerator. The Chieftain shuddered into movement.

'Faster, Ben. We've got to get out of here.'

Ben pressed harder and the tank accelerated. Just then, however, there was an explosion in front of them. Rubble sprayed everywhere, blocking Ben's vision, and he instinctively pulled hard on the right-hand lever. The tank swerved sharply; Ben released the lever to straighten up, but saw himself driving directly towards a hut. He swerved again, missing the building by a whisker. His heart was in his throat as he straightened up once more. In the distance he could see the forest, so he gritted his teeth and pressed the accelerator down full throttle. The tank sped away from the training field and the sound of the bombs grew marginally fainter.

'That,' Annie shouted, 'was a close shave!'

'I think we're clear,' Ben started to say, but before he could finish, something caught his eye. A small box nestled in among the controls in front of him started flashing red. There were words, and he squinted his eyes to read them.

REMOTE CONTROL GUIDANCE SYSTEM. OPERATIONAL.

He blinked, then pulled on one of the levers; it did nothing. He let go of the accelerator; the tank maintained its speed.

'Annie,' he shouted, unable to hide the panic in his voice. 'I've lost control.'

'What?'

'I can't control it. Look!' He pointed at the flashing warning sign. 'Something else has taken control of the tank. I can't steer. I can't stop.'

'I don't believe it,' Annie yelled. '*We're a moving*

213

target! We're being controlled by the RAF for the training exercise! WE'RE A MOVING TARGET!'

And as she spoke, the tank performed a sharp turn. 'We're heading back!' Ben shouted. 'We're heading back to the bombs!'

The roar of the planes and the crash of the explosions grew louder; the ground seemed to tremble.

'Joseph!' Ben shouted. 'You're the scientist. What do we do? How do we get control of the tank again?'

Joseph hauled himself to the front of the tank, but all he could do was stare at the remote control unit. 'I don't know,' he said.

'What do you mean, you don't know?'

'I can't start dismantling it now, Ben.' And as if to confirm what he had just said, the tank was thrown sideways onto one set of wheels, making them tumble around inside. Ben shouted in pain as one of the steering levers dug sharply into his ribs.

'Ben!' Annie called. 'Are you all right?'

'Fine,' Ben growled through gritted teeth. His mind was suddenly clear. The planes were actively targeting them now, but there was no way he was going to give in without a fight. He leaned forward, his body shuddering dramatically from the movement of the tank, and grabbed the box with both hands. He took a deep breath and then, with all his might, tugged on it. The metal dug sharply into the skin of his hands and he hissed with the pain, but rather than let go he tugged again.

And again.

And again.

Finally, with a great heave, he managed to pull the box away from its fittings. A tangled mess of wires sprouted from the back. 'Pull them,' Joseph shouted. 'Just pull the wires as hard as you can.'

Ben did as the old man said. A shower of sparks briefly illuminated the inside of the tank, but for a minute nothing seemed to be happening. The three of them looked at each other with undisguised fear.

And then the tank started to slow down.

'Quick, Ben,' Annie urged. 'Turn us round again.'

Ben didn't need telling. He slammed his foot on the throttle and yanked the right-hand steering lever. The tank almost seemed to skid as it pulled round in a tight turning circle and sped away from the devastation of the training site. Bombs fell left and right. Left and right. The trio remained silent, praying that none of the planes overhead scored a direct hit, holding their breath, every moment fully expecting to be battered to bits.

Eventually, though, Ben became aware that the noise of the training exercise was behind them, but he didn't slow down. Not yet.

Only when they were well clear did he dare to take

his foot off the throttle. The Chieftain ground quickly to a halt, and for a moment they all sat there, listening to the churning sound of the engine turning over, their faces white and their body trembling.

Even above the rumble of the engines, Ben could hear the others' breathing. Heavy. Laboured. But relieved.

'I think we're safe,' Annie gasped.

Ben nodded. 'For now,' he panted. He turned to look at his cousin, and she smiled at him, a bead of sweat trickling down her dirty face.

'Nice driving,' she said.

Chapter Eighteen

How long they sat there, trying to regain their breath and their composure, Ben couldn't have said. It was just a relief to be safe.

Joseph was the first to speak. 'We can't stay here,' he said. 'They will come for us soon. And besides, I need to do something about Vortex.'

Ben turned to look at the old man. The cut and bruises on his face were sore, and there were dark bags under his wild green eyes. He looked to be in a worse state than he had when they first found him, and that was saying something.

'I don't know,' Ben replied nervously. 'Why don't we just try and find someone in charge. Alert them to what's going on.'

Joseph smiled. 'And you think they'll believe you? I've been trying to tell people about strange things happening at Spadeadam for years. Trust me, it's not what they want to hear.'

'Yeah, but *I'm* not—' Ben cut himself short.

'Not mad?' Joseph asked delicately. 'No, I would have to agree with that. But listen to me: Lucian will be scared that other people know of his device. Believe me, Vortex will be leaving that bunker any time now, if it hasn't done already. And if you want to hand yourself over to the RAF, that's up to you. Just make sure you don't accidentally give yourself up to one of Lucian's stooges. It's difficult to tell the difference between friends and enemies in this place, I've noticed.'

'He's right, Ben,' Annie said. 'We can't risk it. And if we're the only people who know about Vortex, we're the ones who have to stop it.'

Ben closed his eyes briefly. His body ached from being thrown around the uncomfortable chassis of the tank; there were already blisters forming on his hands from where he had been tightly gripping the steering handles. But then he looked at Joseph. The old man was a state, his body beaten and bruised. He had taken more punishment than anyone should have been expected to take, let alone a man of his age. Yet Ben knew from a single glance that Joseph would not be deterred from returning to the bunker and doing what- ever was necessary to stop his brother. He also knew that he was in no state to make it there on foot.

'We need to follow the edge of the forest,' he said quietly. 'That was the way we came.'

'Listen to me, you two,' Joseph said. 'You've done enough to help me already. I'm an old man. I can take risks that you two can't. You don't have to help me do this. If you leave now, maybe you can get out of Spadeadam without anyone being the wiser.'

The offer was clearly sincerely meant, but Ben shook his head. 'If Vortex is as bad as you say it is, it's everyone's responsibility.' He looked at Annie. 'Agreed?'

'Agreed.'

'Good. We'll take the tank as far as we can, then continue on foot. Hold tight, everyone.' He pushed his foot down on the throttle, and the tank lurched into movement.

There may have been no planes overhead, but there was a new urgency now – the need to get to the bunker before anything could happen to Vortex. And so Ben sped, full throttle, around the edge of the forest, peering through the viewing hole into the early morning light and hoping that they were heading in the right direction. The other two sat quietly, tensely. None of them knew what was waiting ahead, and a sense of danger seemed to hang in the air around them.

They had been driving for several minutes. Ben's face was creased into an expression of concentration as he did his best to keep to the rough track that skirted round the edge of the forest, when he heard another sound above the growl of the tank's engine. 'What's that?' he asked tersely.

'I'll check,' Annie replied. She held firmly onto the back of Ben's seat, pushed open the circular entrance hatch at the top of the tank, then peered outside.

She ducked back into the relative safety of the tank almost immediately.

'We're being followed!' she yelled. 'Choppers. Two of them. They're overhead!'

'What do we do?' Ben shouted back.

'We have to keep going. They could be regular RAF, but they could be Lucian's men. We can't be sure.'

Suddenly there was an ear-splitting noise, and Ben saw the ground ahead of him explode in a shower of dirt.

'What was that?' he screamed.

'Gunships!' Annie replied. 'It has to be Lucian's people up there! And they're firing at us! We have to get out of the way!' As she spoke, there was another burst of fire from above. 'Get off the track, Ben. Into the woods. They'll hit us any minute, and that's the only place they can't follow.'

Without even thinking, Ben took a deep breath and pulled sharply on the left-hand steering lever. The tank veered towards the forest; as it did so, there was a deafening crackle as bullets ripped into the back of the tank. Ben tried to press harder on the throttle, but it was already fully open: the tank was going as fast as he could make it, and they just had to hope they got under cover in time.

Suddenly all he could see through the viewing window was a massive thicket of trees approaching them. The rat-a-tat of gunship fire outside came in increasingly frenzied bursts.

Crash! The tank trampled over several young saplings on the edge of the forest, crunching them to the ground as easily as skittles being knocked over by a bowling ball. Sweat dripping down his face, Ben saw a thick tree trunk approaching fast out of the gloom. He turned sharply to avoid it and continued several metres across the clearing, before having to yank the vehicle in a different direction.

The trunk that they finally hit seemed to come from nowhere – one moment the way ahead looked clear, the next they were thrown around inside the tank with a sickening thump that seemed to penetrate to the core of their bodies. The engine of the tank started to emit a high-pitched scream as it thrust itself against the tree, an unstoppable force against an immovable object, the tracks around the wheels spinning in the dirt. Ben pulled his foot off the throttle, and the screaming instantly subsided.

'Get out!' he shouted. 'We can't carry on in the

tank – the forest is too thick.'

Immediately, Annie raised her bruised body and pushed the hatch open, before pulling herself up onto the top of the tank. 'Give me your hand, Joseph!' she shouted. She grabbed hold of the old man's bony hand, and Ben helped push him up through the hatch, before pulling himself up onto the top of the metal beast. He glanced towards the front of the machine: the tank gun had been crushed up against the trunk of the massive tree he had hit, which was itself leaning down at an angle from the force of the collision. He jumped down onto the forest floor, then helped Joseph as he painfully dismounted from the tank, followed by Annie – still lithe despite her sore body.

Above them, they could still hear the roar of the helicopter gunships circling overhead. 'We need to get away,' Annie shouted. 'They could land at any minute, then this part of the forest is going to be swarming with them looking for us.'

Ben nodded, then glanced nervously at Joseph. He was in a terrible state, those parts of his face that weren't bruised a deathly white, his breathing laboured. 'Joseph,' he said clearly, 'we need to move quickly. Are you up to it?'

The old man nodded with determination; Ben wasn't convinced.

'We should still follow the edge of the forest,' he

announced. 'My bet is that the guys in the choppers are regular RAF called in to deal with someone trying to steal their tank. They'll expect us to hide deeper in the forest, so it could work to our advantage.'

Annie nodded, and the three of them retraced their steps through the trail of devastation left by the tank, turning away just before they hit the edge of the forest and following the edge of the trees. The buzzing of the choppers – like the sound of enormous wasps out to sting them – grew more distant as they stumbled hurriedly through the trees, occasionally tripping on tree roots, but doing their best to keep going. They couldn't move as fast as they would have liked, however: Joseph was slowing them down. His heavy breathing became more and more laboured, and it wasn't long before his running had become little more than a hurried, limping walk. Finally he misplaced his footing and fell headlong onto the ground.

'Joseph!' Annie cried, but Ben was already there, kneeling down and pulling the old man up.

'Leave me,' he croaked. 'I'm holding you up.'

Ben shook his head. 'No way, Joseph. We've got this far, and we're not giving up now.' He looked over at Annie. 'Help me,' he instructed.

Instinctively she seemed to know what to do. Each of them wrapped one of Joseph's arms around their necks and they helped him move forward, half supporting him, half dragging him through the trees.

It took a good half-hour of struggling in this way before they saw the ominous sight of the hut above the bunker appear through the trees, which were particularly dense here. They stopped, catching their breath and squinting their eyes to see what was going on. There was movement of some kind, but their view was too obscured to see what it was, so they crept as silently as they could to the very edge of the trees, crouching down behind a low bush as they staked the place out.

There were three people there, each of them armed, and a truck with its rear doors flung wide open. Two of them loaded a heavy-looking flight case into the back of the van, while the third stood watch. Even from this distance, Ben could tell it was Flight Lieutenant Johnson. Once the object was loaded into the van, the two soldiers stood in front of Johnson, listening patiently as though receiving instructions of some kind.

'Is that what I think it is?' Annie breathed.

Ben nodded. 'Vortex,' he said. 'It has to be. We can't let that truck leave – at least, we can't let it leave without us on it. If we do, it's over.'

'We need to distract them,' Annie said.

'And quickly,' whispered Joseph. 'Look, they're shutting the doors.'

Ben did it almost without thinking. They needed to

get the three soldiers into the forest – that way they could sneak into the back of the truck without anyone noticing. It was a long shot, but they didn't have the time to think up anything more sophisticated. Ben scrabbled around on the ground and found a couple of good-sized rocks; he threw them out of the forest, making sure that they landed near the soldiers.

'Ben!' Annie hissed. 'What are you doing?'

The three men stopped talking and looked around them, their hands moving automatically to their weapons. Instantly they headed in the direction of Ben, Annie and Joseph; as they approached the forest, Ben heard Johnson ordering them to separate. They did so, while the trio crouched painfully still, barely daring to breathe for fear of alerting the soldiers to their presence. It was touch and go – they only had to stumble across them hiding nervously in the bushes and it would all be over – and every tiny sound they made seemed to be amplified a hundred times.

'There's someone here,' they heard Johnson's voice barking. 'Find them!'

There was a rustling of foliage as the soldiers hunted all around, coming perilously close to the trio's impromptu hiding place.

Ben felt his muscles freezing solid with fear.

They were nearly upon them. They were going to be caught.

He closed his eyes, waiting for the inevitable sensation of an assault rifle poking into his back.

And then the sound of the men faded away, as they searched deeper into the forest.

'Now!' Ben whispered, and the three of them emerged from their hiding place and ran towards the truck – at least, Ben and Annie ran, while Joseph limped – desperately hoping that the soldiers would not call off their search until they had time to secrete themselves in the back of the truck. As soon as they reached the vehicle, Ben opened the back doors and gestured at Joseph and Annie to climb inside. Joseph, however, shook his head.

'What's wrong, Joseph?' Ben asked. 'We haven't got much time.'

'I'm slowing you down,' the old man replied. 'What you have to do is too important for me to be getting in your way.'

'We're not leaving you, Joseph,' Annie said flatly.

Joseph looked piercingly at them, and for a moment time seemed to slow down. 'You are a brave and ingenious couple. I'm sure you'll find a way to destroy that wicked machine.' His eyes flicked towards the hut. 'Besides,' he said, 'I have other things to deal with. They have left the access to the bunker open. I need to go back down there. There are things I need to put an end to.'

Ben looked towards the forest. There was no time for

arguing – the soldiers could return at any moment. 'It's your decision, Joseph,' he said quietly. And then a thought struck him with a dreadful certainty. 'Will we see you again?'

Joseph avoided both Ben's eyes and his question. 'I'm an old man,' he said. 'Who knows what the future holds for me? Who knows what is around the corner?' He looked at the device in the truck. 'Just promise me one thing, Ben,' he said. 'Promise me that you'll destroy that weapon. It must never fall into the wrong hands, do you understand? *Never.*'

'I understand, Joseph.' Ben held out his hand and the old man shook it, before doing the same to Annie, whose eyes were suddenly glassy and tear-filled.

'God's speed,' he whispered. 'And good luck.' He turned and headed straight into the hut, his back stooped but a new sense of purpose in his step. He did not look back.

They watched him disappear, filled with a sense of foreboding. But there was no time to waste on tearful goodbyes. Joseph had given them a job to do; even if he hadn't, their duty was clear.

Without speaking a word, Ben and Annie jumped up into the back of the truck and pulled the doors firmly shut behind them. The flight case was there, firmly attached to the side of the truck with lengths of sturdy rope.

They were alone in the presence of Vortex. It was only a metal case, but somehow it had an aura all of its very own. An aura of fear. And Ben and Annie were the only two people in the world who could do anything to stop it from fulfilling its dreadful destiny.

Chapter Nineteen

Flight Lieutenant Johnson stood in a clearing of trees, his eyes narrowed and his palm firmly gripping the holster of his gun. He was sure he hadn't imagined it. Those stones had fallen barely a few metres away from him, and they hadn't just appeared out of nowhere.

As he looked around him, his two colleagues stumbled upon the clearing. 'Anything?' he asked them curtly, though he needn't have. The very fact that corporals Clarkson and Hildred were here empty-handed made it clear that nobody had found what they were looking for.

The two corporals shook their heads. 'Maybe it was a bird, sir. They drop things from the air sometimes.'

Johnson looked up to see the cloud-scudded sky high above the clearing. Birds – it was certainly a possibility. Even more reason for shooting the pesky things when he saw them. Not that he'd have much more opportunity for that. Vortex would be delivered in a matter of hours; Johnson, Lucian, the two corporals and the handful of others who knew about it would have gone AWOL by then, on a flight out of the country, their bank accounts considerably swollen. No, he had shot his last bird in the Spadeadam countryside, of that he was sure.

'All right,' he mumbled. 'Get back to the truck and start moving. I don't want you to be late.' The three of them hurried back through the forest towards the vehicle, which was just as they had left it.

'You know what to do?' Johnson asked the two men. They nodded. 'Get on with it, then,' he told them, before turning on his heel and heading back into the hut, momentarily cursing himself for leaving the access down to the bunker open. Sloppy, he told himself. Still, soon it wouldn't matter.

Corporals Clarkson and Hildred climbed into the cab of the truck. 'He's one Rupert I won't miss when this is over,' Clarkson moaned as Hildred fired up the ignition.

'Is there any that you will?' Hildred observed, and his colleague laughed ruefully.

'Good point,' he said. He dug his hand into a pocket and pulled out a packet of cigarettes and a cheap plastic lighter. He lit one, took a deep drag, then placed his cigarettes and the lighter on the dashboard as the cab filled with a choking cloud of smoke.

Their instructions were clear: to take their cargo across country to a warehouse near the port in Newcastle. Once they had handed over the device as arranged, they would dump the truck and immediately take a ferry to Amsterdam, then on to a private airfield where false passports would be waiting for them, along with a plane that would transport them to South Africa. Once they were there, they would be on their own.

But first things first: they needed to get out of Spadeadam without attracting the attention of their idiot RAF colleagues, and onto the open road. They drove in silence, dreaming of the money that was about to come their way, and the things they would do with it.

'What was that?' Clarkson asked suddenly.

'What?'

'Something's banging.'

Hildred listened. 'I can't hear anything,' he said. But even as he spoke there was an unmistakable knocking sound from the back of the truck.

'Hear it?'

'Yeah, I heard it.' He put his foot on the brake and the truck pulled gently to a halt. 'Did you strap the thing in properly?'

'You saw me do it,' Clarkson replied.

'Well, maybe it's come loose. We'd better check.' They left the engine turning over as they jumped down from the cab and walked to the back of the truck.

Clarkson put his hand to the door handle and clicked it open. 'It's probably noth—'

As he spoke, his side of the door sprang open and crunched harshly into his face. He shouted in pain as he put his hands up to his face and felt blood instantly pouring from his nose; he was barely even aware of the other door bursting open and whacking Hildred equally hard. Blinded by the sudden pain, they couldn't see who it was that had suddenly attacked them; but they were certainly aware of the flurry of kicks and punches that landed on their knees and in their stomach, forcing them onto the dirty ground, groaning in agony.

'They're down!' a female voice shouted. 'Get in the front!'

'No!' another voice barked – a male this time, but young. 'Get their guns first.' Another blow in the stomach, and their weapons were forcibly taken from them.

They heard the doors slam shut, and with a shock of realization the implication of what was happening dawned on Clarkson. 'Vortex!' he shouted, pushing himself up to his knees. But his eyes were full of blood and he could barely see, let alone do anything about what was happening. And as he scrabbled around in the dirt, a billow of exhaust fumes blew into his face, causing him to cough and splutter.

'Stop them!' he heard Hildred shouting. '*Stop them!*'

But it was too late. The engine of the truck had roared into life, and by the time either of them could see again, it had already driven off, and was speeding into the distance.

Ben was no expert at driving a truck, but after his exploits in the Congo he was good enough. The gears crunched noisily as he shifted them up as quickly as possible and sped away from the two soldiers they had just overcome, completely against the odds. They sped along the road in anxious silence. There was nothing to say – they both knew the stakes. The soldiers whose places they had taken most likely had mobile phones on them; they would already have been in touch with Lucian's people, and the chase would be on. Ben and Annie's hastily cobbled together plan was falling apart at the seams.

The truck hit a bump in the road, shaking them about and causing something to fall off the dashboard.

'What was that?' Ben asked tensely, keeping his eye on the road ahead and not daring to look in the side mirrors to see if anyone was following them.

'Just a packet of cigarettes,' Annie replied. 'And a lighter.'

Ben blinked. A lighter. An idea began to form in his mind. 'Hold on,' he told his cousin, before clenching his jaw and turning the steering wheel into a sharp left turn. The truck left the road and juddered across country a little distance before he slammed down the brakes and brought them to an abrupt stop. The engine shuddered, and then stalled.

'What are we doing?' Annie asked.

'Get out,' Ben told her. 'And bring the lighter.'

They jumped out of the cab and ran round to the back of the truck, which Ben opened. Vortex was still there, safely entombed in its metal flight case and still tied to the truck with ropes.

'We can't open the flight case,' Ben said, thinking out loud. 'We already tried that, and it's useless without the key. It's too heavy for us to carry it anywhere, and they'll already have sent someone after us. We've only got one option, and that's to destroy the thing here and now.'

'How, Ben? It's a metal flight case. You're not going to set fire to it with a plastic lighter.'

Ben shook his head. 'I've got another idea. Here, give me a hand.'

They climbed up into the back of the truck.

'Undo the rope,' he said. 'We need the longest piece we can find.'

Annie looked panicked and confused, but she had

234

no option other than to do what Ben said. The knots that fastened the flight case to the side of the truck were large, thick and difficult to untie; and the fact that they were rushing meant it seemed to take even longer to loosen them. Eventually, however, they did untie them. Unravelling the rope, they managed to unwind a piece that was at least ten metres long. Ben looked at it unenthusiastically. 'It'll have to do,' he murmured to himself.

'What do you mean, it'll have to do?' Annie demanded. 'What's going on, Ben?'

But there was no time to explain. They jumped down, then Ben grabbed the keys that were still in the ignition and unlocked the fuel cap at the back of the truck. 'Give me the rope,' he told Annie.

She handed it to him, and he carefully started to thread it into the fuel tank. 'We need to get it saturated,' he said tensely.

'Ben!' Annie warned. 'Look!'

He glanced in the direction that she was pointing. In the distance were two more trucks coming towards them. It was clear that they were moving very quickly.

Half the rope had been fed into the fuel tank by now, so Ben pulled it out, then started to insert the other end.

'They're getting nearer, Ben! I don't know what

you've got planned but it had better work – these people have already tried to kill us once today.'

'Just a few more seconds.' His hands were covered in stinking diesel as he continued to feed in the rope.

'Hurry!'

It was done. The whole rope was saturated. Ben started to pull it out, leaving a little of the diesel-soaked rope hanging inside the fuel tank; the rest of it he laid out on the ground, pulling it in a straight line so that the end was as far away from the truck as possible.

'Give me the lighter, Annie,' he said quietly.

Annie's eyes widened as she realized what he was planning to do. 'It's too dangerous,' she said. 'We're too close.'

'Get away from the truck.'

She stood firm.

'Annie, you heard what Joseph said. If we don't destroy this thing, thousands of people could die. This is a real Code Red situation. *Now get away from the truck.*'

'No,' she replied.

'Annie, they'll be here in a couple of minutes. Give me the lighter – it's the only chance we've got.'

'No, Ben,' she said. 'Look at your hands – they're covered with fuel. If you spark up that lighter, you might go up in flames yourself.'

'I'm going to have to risk it.'

'No you're not, Ben.' She held out her arms. 'My hands are clean. I can do it.'

'*Annie!*' he said urgently. 'We haven't got time to argue.'

'Then you'd better do what I say.' She stared defiantly at him – one of those stares that Ben knew he couldn't argue against.

'All right,' he said quietly. 'But I'm staying with you. The moment the flame touches the end of the rope, we run – OK?'

Annie nodded. They could hear the engines of the approaching trucks now; there wasn't a single second to lose. 'Ready?'

'Ready. Good luck, Annie.' He clasped hold of her free hand as she bent down and sparked the cigarette lighter into flame.

'Annie,' Ben said. 'I'm sorry I dragged you into this. I'm sorry I forced you to come into Spadeadam.'

His cousin looked at him. 'Don't be silly, Ben. Do you really think I wanted to be left behind?'

A slow grin spread over Ben's face. 'Not really,' he said.

They both looked back down and held their breath. 'Ready?'

'Ready!'

Annie lit the rope.

'*Run!*' Ben shouted. Hand in hand they sprinted as fast as they could away from the truck.

It was a matter of seconds before it exploded. Ben and Annie were thrown to the ground by an intense blast of burning air, and they covered their heads with their arms to shield themselves from the chunks of burning shrapnel that flew all around them. As the explosion subsided, there was a flaming crackle, and Ben turned over onto his back to see the vehicle burning, a thick black stream of smoke rising up into the air.

'We did it!' Annie said breathlessly. 'We destroyed it.'

But Ben didn't answer. Instead he squinted his eyes and looked through the flames into the wavering distance beyond. The vehicles that had been following him were there, and three soldiers had climbed down. They looked at the burning truck with unconcealed horror, and Ben realized that what they saw was not a burning weapon, but the piles of money they were expecting to get paid, all going up in smoke. In an instant they all started shouting at each other.

'That's right,' Ben whispered to himself. 'Keep arguing. Keep arguing, then get back in your trucks and drive away.'

It was a vain hope. From the midst of their increasingly heated discussion, one of the soldiers happened to look past the flames. His eyes widened as he saw Ben and Annie lying there.

'Look!' they heard him shout as he pointed in their direction. His colleagues stopped arguing and glanced over. And then, without hesitation, they sprinted towards them.

Ben and Annie moved as one. They jumped to their feet and started running through the high grass away from the soldiers.

They dared not look back, and they dared not slow down. Only their legs could save them now.

Chapter Twenty

Joseph walked implacably down the concrete corridor.

He knew there wasn't much time. Not because of Ben and Annie and what they had to do, but because of himself. The pressure was building up inside his head; his hands were shaking; he was becoming enshrouded in the black cloak of paranoia. He recognized the warning signs of a psychotic episode only too well. It would happen in minutes or hours; but he knew it would happen. He had to get to Lucian before the shadow fell over his mind and he became helpless.

But first there was something he had to find.

He had seen it before, when he was with the others and they were peering into rooms in this underground warren. He had made a mental note then, but trying to find his way around this maze was an impossibility. He'd know the room when he stumbled upon it, of course, but until then he had only one option: to try every door he came across, and hope that he didn't run into any of the men his brother was commanding to help him in his twisted plan.

The last three rooms he had looked into had been empty. Keep focused, Joseph, he kept telling himself. It won't be long now. You're nearly there. Keep focused.

He stopped, thinking he had heard footsteps. Maybe he had, maybe he hadn't. Maybe they were in his mind. It felt like people were watching him. 'Maybe they *are* watching you, Joseph,' a voice seemed to say in his head in a light, sing-song way.

He clenched his jaw. 'Get out of my head,' he said out loud. 'You're not there. You don't exist.'

And once again he was surrounded by silence.

Joseph looked around. He had stopped by another door, the only one in the particularly gloomy corridor in which he found himself. He listened carefully to check there was nobody talking on the other side; when he heard nothing, he opened it and peered in.

When he saw what was inside, he smiled to himself. He stepped into the room and closed the door behind him.

There was a light switch on the wall – a very old-fashioned one – and it illuminated a single bulb hanging from the ceiling. On the far wall of the room was a mass of metal shelving, groaning with equipment. The right-hand side contained electrical equipment – wire, switches, batteries. The left-hand side housed several large boxes. On a number of these, written in red letters, were the words Joseph had been looking for: 'DANGER: SEMTEX.'

He knew why Lucian needed to have Semtex. The plastic explosive was used to harden steel that had a high manganese percentage – no doubt that was what he had used to make the components of his terrible weapon. But Joseph had a very different use for it. A more destructive use. A use that would ensure that Vortex could never be remade. At least, not by Lucian.

Without hesitation, he went to work.

Making the radio-controlled switch would not prove to be an intellectual difficulty for the old man; what made it harder was the fact that his hands were still shaking, and the equipment he had found required certain adjustments. He soon managed it though, and then he turned his attention to the plastic explosive. He was going to require a large amount of Semtex, and something to carry it in. His eyes fell upon a small silver flight case. He opened it up to discover that it was empty. That would do.

Minutes later, he had loaded several pounds of Semtex into the case. He inserted the two electrical probes of his makeshift detonator into the plastic explosive, closed the case, and then picked up the detonator control he had just instructed.

Once that was done, he allowed himself a moment's silence. His last moment, before he took the greatest risk of his life: the risk of turning himself into a dead man walking.

He took the push-button switch firmly in his right hand, and without further hesitation pressed it down. The moment he released it, the Semtex would explode, and there was enough of the stuff to bring down the whole bunker.

With grim determination, he picked the flight case up in the other hand, then stepped out into the corridor.

'Release it,' the voice said in his head, but Joseph ignored it. It took a great effort of will, but he ignored it. Instead, he started to shout at the top of his voice. 'Where is Lucian?' he bellowed. 'Take me to him. Take me to him now!'

Several times he called, and his voice echoed around the concrete corridors. It did not take long for him to hear the hurried patter of footsteps approaching, and this time he knew without question that they were real, not figments of his damaged imagination. Seconds later, two soldiers came running up the corridor towards him, assault rifles at the ready.

'Get on the floor,' one of them shouted.

'I won't be doing that,' Joseph replied. He held the switch in the air. 'The moment I let go of this, several pounds of high-grade plastic explosive packed into this case will explode.'

The soldiers' eyes widened.

'You must understand that I don't want to harm you, but I *will* release it unless you do exactly what I say. Do you understand?'

'Y-y-yes,' the soldiers stuttered.

'Good. Now take me immediately to Lucian.'

The soldiers nodded, turned and started to walk down the corridor.

'Not so quickly,' Joseph instructed. 'I'm an old man. I cannot keep up.' The soldiers steadied their pace a little, though they still walked with agitation, throwing nervous glances back at Joseph as they led him along the maze of corridors to Lucian's room. Once there, they knocked.

'What is it?' Lucian's voice called impatiently.

The soldiers walked in, followed by Joseph.

'What do you wa—?' Lucian's question faltered as he saw his brother enter the room.

He was wearing a brown overcoat, and had a briefcase on the table. Flight Lieutenant Johnson was with him. They looked as if they were just preparing to leave, but when Lucian's eyes fell on his brother, he was unable to hide his shock.

'I thought you were—' he started to say.

'Sir!' one of the soldiers interrupted. 'You have to listen to me. He's got a bomb. He has Semtex loaded in that case, and he's carrying a detonator.'

'He's right, Lucian,' Joseph agreed.

Silence fell on the room.

'He's bluffing,' Flight Lieutenant Johnson whispered.

Lucian ignored his sidekick. 'Show me the explosives, Joseph,' he said calmly.

Slowly, his hands still shaking, Joseph placed the flight case on the table and opened it. Lucian's lips went thin when he saw the huge amount of Semtex that was loaded inside. He nodded his head slowly.

'Don't do anything foolish, Joseph,' he said carefully. 'We can sort this out. We can come to an arrangement.'

'An arrangement?' Flight Lieutenant Johnson hissed. 'What are you talking about. He's a madman.'

'*Shut up!*' Lucian shouted.

Joseph ignored his abrasive brother. Instead he turned to Johnson. 'A madman?' he murmured. 'So they have been telling me for many years. But there are different kinds of madness, are there not? The madness that inspires someone to develop a weapon that could kill millions, for example. There are enough such weapons in the world, without madmen creating more.' He glanced at Lucian as he spoke, then turned to the two soldiers. 'How long do you need to evacuate this bunker?' he asked.

The soldiers looked at each other. 'Five minutes,' one of them said uncertainly.

'You've got three,' he said, before turning to Johnson. 'You, go with them. Get everyone out and well away from the area. Do you understand?'

White-faced and sweating, Johnson nodded his head.

'*Go!*'

The three of them left, leaving Joseph alone, finally, with his brother.

Ben's muscles were burning.

He and Annie were sprinting as fast as they could, both of them easily matched as far as speed was concerned; but the men following them had longer legs and were catching up.

'Don't stop,' he gasped at Annie. 'If we stop, they'll either catch us or shoot us.'

Annie didn't reply, but her look of agonized exhaustion as she continued to run alongside him said it all. She was feeling the same pain throughout her body that Ben was; she too was at the mercy of her willpower as they struggled to break through the pain barrier and reach the forest up ahead where at least they would have a chance of hiding. A chance of surviving.

Ben allowed himself a quick glance over his shoulder as he ran. The soldiers were further behind than he thought, which gave him a surge of momentary relief. They had stopped. But then he saw why. One of the soldiers raised his weapon and pointed it in their direction.

'Get down!' he screamed at Annie, pulling her heavily to the earth even as he spoke. They hit the ground just in time – a shot echoed around the countryside, and Ben was sure he heard the bullet whizzing over his head. Looking back, he saw the men had started to run towards them again.

'We need to keep going,' he said breathlessly. 'Run in a zigzag – it'll make us a more difficult target.'

'It'll slow us down too,' Annie puffed.

'Yeah, but I've got an idea.' They started to run again, weaving in and out. As they did, Ben reached into his combat trousers and pulled out the gun he had taken from the soldier driving the truck. 'I hope this thing's loaded,' he gasped, before turning to look at the men following. He flicked off the safety catch, stretched out his hand, aimed just above the heads of the three men chasing them, and fired two deafening shots.

The men shouted in surprise and alarm, then hit the ground. Ben and Annie upped the pace, ignoring the shrieking pain from their muscles. They had to get to the forest, and quickly.

Behind them, the soldiers pushed themselves up to their feet, but no sooner had they done so than Ben fired another couple of shots, forcing them back down to the ground.

'We're nearly there!' Annie shouted. 'We're nearly at the trees!'

A shot rang out behind them.

'*Keep going!*' Ben yelled, and with gritted teeth they made a final spurt for cover, crashing into the forest with an explosive breath of relief.

'We need to hide,' Annie gasped. 'But where?'

Ben looked around them. He knew they only had seconds to make a decision.

'Here,' he said. He looked up – the canopy above him was thick. 'Our best bet is to climb up a tree on the edge,' he said. 'Even if they expect us to do that, there are hundreds of trees here, so it will be nearly impossible for them to find us. Follow me.'

They ran along the edge of the forest a little way until they found a tree suitable for climbing. 'You go first,' he urged Annie, then watched as she scaled the tree with cat-like skill. Within seconds she was hidden in the upper branches. Ben tucked the gun back into his combat trousers, then launched himself at the tree trunk, following the route that his cousin had so deftly taken. There were plenty of footholds, and he was several metres up before he heard the sound of voices nearby. He looked above him – not far now until he was out of sight – and kicked his foot into the next foothold to propel himself upwards. As he did, however, the gun slipped and fell to the ground. The moment it hit the earth, the weapon went off with a loud bang that nearly caused Ben to lose his grip and fall from the tree.

'What was that?' he heard someone shout. The voice was much closer than he had expected, and he scrambled desperately to the top of the tree, where Annie was waiting for him, her face white with concern.

'What happened?' she whispered.

'The gun,' Ben replied. 'I dropped it.'

More voices from below. It was difficult to tell exactly where they came from, but they weren't far away, that much was sure.

'If they find it—' Annie breathed.

'I know,' Ben replied. 'If they find it, they'll realize where we are.' He looked seriously at his cousin. 'I'm sorry, Annie,' he said. 'I don't see a way out. If these people think we know about Vortex, they're going to want to silence us.'

He looked around uselessly. In the distance, through the trees, they could see the remains of the burning truck where the ruins of the device were slowly melting away; and beyond that he thought he could make out the hut that concealed the entrance to the underground bunker where they had left Joseph.

Poor Joseph. So keen to confront his wicked brother, he would be at Lucian's mercy yet again. Ben shuddered to think about it, before snapping back to their own predicament. He could hear people moving around at the bottom of the tree.

'The gun,' he heard a voice say. 'The kid must have dropped it. They must have climbed up here.'

Ben closed his eyes. 'It looks like Joseph's not the only person who has no more places to run to . . .' he whispered.

A minute passed, and neither Joseph nor Lucian spoke. The two brothers just looked at each other, drinking in the sight of the faces that they had not seen for so long.

'I don't want to kill you, Lucian,' Joseph said finally. 'But you will do as I say, or I *will* detonate the bomb.'

'What is that you want me to do, Joseph?' Lucian asked tersely. A bead of sweat ran down his face.

'I want you to come with me. We will leave the case of Semtex here, and together we will walk out of this place. I want you to promise me that you will never again use your knowledge to devise something that will harm so many people, and I'm going to trust you to keep that promise, though I do not know what you have done to deserve such trust. We will then destroy this place, so all the remnants of your work will be gone.'

Joseph's ultimatum hung in the air between them.

'You need to take control of yourself, Joseph,' Lucian said after a moment, his voice trembling slightly. 'I know you're angry, but this isn't the solution.'

Joseph clutched his finger down firmly on the detonator. 'What you mean, of course, is that it isn't *your* solution,' he replied.

'It's the solution of an unhinged mind,' Lucian said sharply. 'Fight it, Joseph. Fight it, and think.' He took a step closer. 'You are struggling with your demons. I can see it in your face. Let me help you.'

'Take another step towards me, Lucian, and I will release my thumb without hesitation.'

Lucian trod carefully backwards.

'Fifty years,' Joseph continued. 'Fifty years you stole from me the day you decided that I would be a suitable subject for your experiments.'

'They weren't experiments, Joseph. We knew what the drugs would do. We were saving you from yourself. Do you really believe we were working alone? The intelligence services knew what we were doing, and if you had blown the whistle they would have killed you. My way was much better. It was for your own good.'

'My own good?' Joseph smiled, and appeared to be

thinking for a moment. 'You're right. My mind is clouding over. It has been for the last few days. Occasionally I snap out of it, but soon I will be out of control. It's my medication, you see. I don't have it, and without my medication, the world is a dark and frightening place.'

Lucian's eyes narrowed, and Joseph could see hope in his face.

'But the clouds have not yet fully descended,' he continued. 'Some things are clear, and one of them is this: that if there is one person in the whole world who is not fit to judge what is for anyone's own good, it is you, my brother.' He spat the final word with distaste. 'But I am giving you a final chance – a chance to redeem yourself.'

Lucian's lip curled into a sneer. 'Redeem myself? If you believe that I want redemption, you are stupid as well as insane. You have no idea of what I have done. You have no idea of the things my mind has achieved.'

'Ah,' Joseph purred, 'Vortex, you mean? A grand name for such an evil device. I'm sorry to tell you, however, that by now Vortex will be destroyed, or at the very least in safe hands.'

Lucian blinked. 'Destroyed?' he repeated. 'Impossible. It's on its way to the delivery point as we speak.'

Joseph shook his head. 'Not if Ben and Annie have anything to do with it,' he said softly.

'Ben and Annie?' Lucian laughed. 'Those kids? Don't be ridiculous.'

Joseph shrugged. 'Clearly I have more confidence in them than you do. All this, however, is rather academic. I am going to destroy this place, Lucian. Whether or not you come with me is up to you.'

A tiny smile of triumph flickered over Lucian's face. 'But you won't leave me alone with the bomb, Joseph,' he taunted. 'You know I will just remove the detonator. If you try and kill me, you'll kill yourself in the process.'

Joseph raised an eyebrow. 'All that intellect, my brother, and you truly suppose that that hadn't crossed my mind?'

Lucian's eyes narrowed. 'You won't do it,' he whispered. 'You won't sacrifice your life to get back at me.'

'To get back at you, Lucian? Haven't you been listening to a word I've said? What I'm doing is not to get back at you. It's to protect the thousands of innocent lives that you would destroy if you were left unchecked.'

He closed his eyes briefly, then looked back at Lucian. His brother was scared now. Terrified. It gave him no pleasure, but there it was.

'Besides,' Joseph said, his voice cracked now, and trembling, 'do you call this hollow existence you have left me with a *life*?'

The question remained unanswered as a wave of indecision crashed over Lucian's face.

'Please, Lucian,' Joseph begged. 'Please. You know what the right thing to do is. This can end now. I don't want revenge, and I forgive you for what you have done. Make the right decision, Lucian, for once in your life.'

His brother was looking down at the floor now, his shoulders slumped. Finally, he moved his head up. His lips were thin; his face was white.

'OK, Joseph,' he whispered, his voice suddenly frail, betraying his age. 'You win. I'll come with you.' And with that, the elderly scientist stepped towards his brother. As he walked past the suitcase he paused, as though contemplating doing something; but a quick glance at Joseph, his finger firmly on the detonating button, clearly persuaded him otherwise.

Joseph looked towards the door. 'You go first,' he said. 'I'll follow.'

Lucian nodded, and stepped towards the door.

What made Lucian do it, Joseph would never find out. Perhaps he thought he could overcome his brother; perhaps the thought of his laboratory being destroyed, with all the research and secrets that it contained, was too much for him. Whatever the reason, as he approached his brother, Lucian hurled himself towards Joseph. They fell heavily to the ground, and Joseph felt his brother's hand clasp firmly over his own, pressing down on his thumb so that he could not release the button.

'Get up!' Lucian hissed as they struggled on the floor. 'Get up and walk to the suitcase. We're going to disengage that detonator.'

Lucian had the upper hand, and with all his might he dragged Joseph up to his feet. 'You're as crazy as you ever were,' he whispered as he did so.

The old men staggered slightly as they stood up. Joseph found that the room was spinning, and it was all he could do to keep his attention focused on his button thumb, which Lucian was keeping firmly pressed down. But as they edged awkwardly towards the flight case, their legs became tangled and they tripped. As they fell, Joseph's head cracked hard on the corner of the table.

Instantly he went limp and lost consciousness.

Lucian fell too, pulled to the floor by the dead weight of his unconscious brother. And as he did so, he lost all sense of co-ordination. His knees buckled, and his hand slipped from over the thumb of his brother.

The detonating button made a small click as it was released, and that click was the last sound Lucian Sinclair ever heard.

Chapter Twenty-one

'We know you're there!' the soldier's voice called up from the ground.

Silence.

'You've got two options. Climb down quietly, or have us shoot you down, like birds.'

Ben and Annie glanced at each other, and each of them shook their head. If the soldiers wanted them, they'd have to come and get them.

'I'm going to count to five,' the soldier shouted. 'If you're not down by then, we open fire. One.'

Ben gripped onto the bark of the tree. It hurt his hand he was holding on so hard.

'Two.'

Annie looked frightened. Ben didn't blame her: he was frightened too.

'Three.'

There was a barely audible click from below as the soldier readied his weapon. Ben bit his lip, desperately trying to think of a plan.

But they never heard him say 'Four', because suddenly there was an immense explosion. It was in the distance, clearly, but it was loud enough to make startled birds rise out of the trees in great flocks, squawking with alarm.

'What was that?' one of the soldiers shouted. Even as he spoke, however, Ben and Annie looked sharply at each other and whispered one word.

'Joseph.'

From their vantage point at the top of the tree, they looked back towards the bunker. A huge black pall of smoke was hovering above it, and the whole place was a scene of devastation. Ben squinted his eyes – he thought he could see figures running away from the area. Somehow he knew, without quite understanding how, that neither Lucian nor Joseph would be one of those figures.

Below them, the soldiers had started to talk heatedly.

'The bunker – it's blown!'

'We have to get away from here. This place is going to be crawling with people before we know it.'

'No,' another voice said harshly. 'Those kids know about Vortex. If they tell anyone . . .'

'Then what? Vortex has been destroyed. So has the

bunker. There's no evidence it ever existed. Let's just get out of here before any of our colleagues ask us what we're doing. We can forget about our money, if that's what's worrying you.'

'I agree,' said a third voice.

'Listen, I'm the ranking officer here. I'm giving you an order.'

'You can give us as many orders as you like. What are you going to do, court martial us? We're getting out of here.'

As he spoke, a mobile phone rang. The ranking officer answered, then listened silently to whoever was at the other end of the phone. 'Get back to barracks,' he instructed. 'Now.' He clicked the phone shut. 'Lucian,' he said to the others. 'He was in the bunker when it blew. He's dead.'

There was a brief pause, then one of the other soldiers spoke. 'We really have got to get out of here then. There are going to be questions, and we don't want to have to answer them.'

A moment later, through the treetops, Ben saw the three soldiers leaving. They ran back to the waiting trucks, and drove off out of sight. Half of him wanted to breathe a sigh of relief, but he couldn't bring himself to do so. Instead he found his eyes fixed on the cloud of smoke drifting away from the bunker.

'There was a room of explosives down there,' he said

numbly. 'Joseph must have found it and . . .' His voice trailed away. In the past couple of days he had gone from fearing Joseph to respecting him; he couldn't bear to think of the old man meeting his final moments in that hated underground bunker.

'Maybe he wasn't down there,' Annie said quietly. 'Maybe he escaped.'

'Yeah,' Ben replied. 'Maybe.' Deep down he knew the truth.

They fell silent and continued to watch the smoke as it drifted across the wild Spadeadam landscape.

How long they sat there, uncomfortable among the upper branches of the tree, Ben didn't know. He was too busy thinking about Joseph. Had it really only been a couple of days ago that they first saw him, alone and haunting on the bridge of the railway station? He had seemed so mysterious then, mysterious and scary. And that hadn't really changed, Ben realized as he thought about it. All that had changed was that they had started to understand him a bit better. Maybe that was why the old man had seemed to trust them. For fifty years, nobody had taken him seriously; for fifty years his ramblings had been dismissed as the paranoia of a madman.

If only it hadn't ended like this.

'He shouldn't have done that,' Annie interrupted his thoughts.

'What?'

'Joseph. He killed his brother. There must have been another way. There's *always* another way.' Her voice sounded tearful as she spoke, and Ben couldn't tell if she was angry with the old man, or sad for him.

'Yes,' Ben muttered. 'Yes, I suppose you're right.' But in his heart he wasn't so sure. It was unavoidable, what Joseph had done; and it was true that innocent people could have been hurt in the explosion. But what if Lucian had rebuilt Vortex? What then?

Sometimes, he realized, things were not black and white. They were shades of grey.

And what was it Lucian had said was the motto of Spadeadam? *Si vis pacem, para bellum.* If you wish for peace, prepare for war. He continued to stare at the scene of destruction. Joseph, he finally understood, had been fighting a war in his mind for most of his life. What they had just witnessed was the final battle; only now was he at peace.

Ben took a deep breath, and turned his attention back to Annie.

'What that soldier just said was right,' he told her. 'It won't be long before this place is crawling with RAF. If they catch us, we're going to have some pretty awkward explaining to do.'

'Like what?' Annie asked.

'Like what we were doing wrecking one of their

tanks. Like what we were doing blowing up one of their trucks.' He glanced back towards the bunker. 'Like what we had to do with what's going on over there. Listen, Annie, I don't think we're out of trouble yet. Any evidence to do with Vortex has been destroyed; the people involved will deny all knowledge of it. If we try and tell the authorities, they'll never believe us – they'll think that we're just making it all up, that we're trying to wriggle out of what we've been up to here. We're compromised, Annie. We're in a corner. Even your dad wouldn't be able to get us out of this.'

'But we've done a good thing, Ben. We've . . . we've saved lives, haven't we?'

'I know, Annie. And I know it bites, but we're just going to have to keep it to ourselves.'

Annie's eyes widened as the truth of Ben's words struck her. 'So what do we do?' she breathed.

'There's only one thing we can do. Try and get out of here without being caught. Nobody knows our names; if we can get back to the youth hostel without being collared, nobody will be any the wiser.'

'Do you think we should go now, before the RAF get here?' But as she spoke, there was another noise in the background that answered their question. They peered out from the foliage to see two helicopters approaching. 'They're the same choppers that chased us earlier,' Annie murmured. They landed at a safe distance from the burning bunker, and as their doors opened, a swarm of armed RAF men jumped out. Suddenly there were trucks everywhere, driving up the road to examine the burning vehicle and erecting a human perimeter around the area of devastation.

'I guess that's a no,' Annie whispered.

'We'll have to wait till dark,' Ben said. 'It's our only chance of sneaking out unseen.'

Annie nodded. 'Makes sense,' she said. 'But we've got a long time to wait.' She re-manoeuvred her body against the harsh bark of the tree. 'And this isn't the place I'd choose to be hanging around.'

The day passed unbearably slowly. Ben and Annie kept watch on the movement of the RAF and the emergency services who were swarming around the site – half to distract them from how uncomfortable they were, half because they wanted to keep tabs on where everyone was before they tried to make their escape.

Morning turned to afternoon, and afternoon to evening. They tried not to think about how long it had been since they had eaten, and their lips seemed to stick together with thirst. As the light began to fail, Ben grew increasingly anxious, and he could tell that the same was true for Annie. Helicopters and trucks were still all over the place, their powerful lights beaming out into the countryside. Ben had the distinct impression that they were looking for something – or someone. Anyone.

'They probably think it's a terrorist attack,' he whispered.

Annie nodded mutely.

'Still, we can't stay up here for days. I reckon we've got another twenty minutes of light. As soon as it's dark, we go, OK?'

'OK.'

The day might have been slow, but the next twenty minutes passed more quickly than Ben would have liked. Almost before he knew it, it was fully dark and they were preparing to leave. Ben descended first, stepping over the gun that was still lying at the foot of the tree – that was the last time he wanted to see a weapon of any kind for a long time – then waited for Annie to join him. Then, treading carefully in the treacherous dark, they started trekking deeper into the forest, away from the focal point of activity. It seemed strange, walking in the opposite direction from where they had left Joseph, almost as though they were deserting him; but Joseph had chosen his own path, and there was nothing they could do about that now.

They walked blindly in the silence and the dark, their hands held in front of them to stop themselves from bumping into trees. Neither Ben nor Annie had any idea where they were going, and soon they were wildly disorientated.

The sounds were strange in the forest. The sounds of night. Wild animals called to each other, and there was mysterious shuffling all around them. All they could do was ignore it and press on, hoping that they would come out of the forest on the other side and find some way of orientating themselves. They held hands in order to stop themselves from getting separated; more than once, one of them tripped and had to be held up by the other. It was a frightening journey.

Gradually, however, they became aware that the trees were starting to thin. Desperate to be out of the forest, they upped their pace; in the end they practically ran, hand in hand, out of the woods and onto the grassland beyond. Ben blinked. The moon was startlingly bright – so bright, in fact, that it cast shadows on the ground as sharp and distinct as if it were a summer's day. They stood for a moment, breathing heavily with relief, only now admitting to themselves how scared they had been in the woods. Once they had calmed down, Ben started to look around.

'Over there,' he said, pointing away from them. 'The boundary fence.'

Instinctively, they started running towards it. But they had only moved a few metres when Annie called to him.

'Ben! Stop!'

His heart jumped. 'What is it?'

He turned to look at Annie, expecting the worst.

But his cousin's face had a mysterious smile as she pointed up into the sky. There, silhouetted against the fat, silvery moon, they could see the shadow of a bird, swooping gracefully in the night sky. Time seemed to stand still as they watched it, solitary and magnificent, unaware that it was being admired, and unworried, for the moment at least, by the presence of humans.

'What is it?' Ben whispered.

'I don't know,' Annie replied. 'An owl of some kind. But whatever it is, it's beautiful.'

And so it was. The two cousins continued to watch it until suddenly, without warning, it drifted away on some unseen eddy of wind, leaving Ben and Annie alone once more.

They stood together in a kind of respectful silence, aware that they had been privileged to share that moment with the mysterious, phantom-like bird. Ben found himself wondering if Annie, too, was thinking about Joseph, and how he had entered briefly into their lives and then, like the bird, disappeared, never to be seen again.

He didn't ask her. Instead he took her by the hand.

'Come on,' he said quietly. 'Let's get home.'

And hand in hand, they tramped out of Spadeadam and along the boundary fence. They did not look back until they reached the warmth and safety of the youth hostel, where they slept more deeply than they had ever slept before.

Epilogue

Three days later

Ben's body ached from the bruises he had sustained in the tank, but he ignored them as he jumped down off the bus and hurried along the street to Annie's house. In his hand he clutched an A4 envelope, and he wanted to show his cousin the contents.

He rapped on the front door and Annie answered. She nodded at him, and silently led him upstairs to her bedroom. The bird magazine that Annie had showed him last time he was here was lying on her bed, open at the page that showed the picture of the hen harrier. Ben felt a pang as he remembered seeing the birds being shot down, but also a small surge of pride that maybe – just maybe – they had made the world a little bit safer for those birds that remained.

As soon as they had shut the door behind them, Ben spoke. 'I've got something to show you,' he said, and he handed over the envelope.

Annie looked curiously inside, and pulled out a piece of paper. It was a photocopy of a newspaper cutting, and the two of them read it together.

It was only a small article, and the picture that accompanied it was faint. There was no mistaking the face though – the hooked nose, the floppy hair, the piercing stare. It was Joseph. A young Joseph, but Joseph nevertheless. They read the words that accompanied it in silence.

```
A physicist, Joseph Sinclair, has been
detained indefinitely at a hospital for
the mentally ill in York. Mr Sinclair, 21,
was widely viewed as one of the most
promising young scientists of his gener-
ation, but friends had become increasingly
concerned about his erratic behaviour in
recent weeks. His brother, Lucian
Sinclair, spoke of his family's concerns.
'We are desperately worried for Joseph,'
he told this newspaper, 'but we are
confident he will make a full recovery in
the very near future.'
```

Annie breathed deeply. 'It's horrible, isn't it,' she said,

'what people are willing to do to each other?'

Ben nodded.

'Do you think he knew?' she asked him. 'What he was doing, I mean, when he blew up the bunker? Or was it the voices in his head that he told us about?'

'I don't know, Annie,' he replied. 'I guess we'll never know.'

Before he could say anything else, there was a knock at the door.

'Come in,' Annie called.

The door opened, and a tall, thickset man with steely grey hair appeared.

Annie blinked, then smiled. 'Dad!' she said with delight, then ran to her father, who embraced her in a great bear hug.

Air Commodore James Macpherson smiled at Ben over his daughter's shoulder. 'Ben,' he greeted him affably.

'Hi, James,' Ben replied. He barely ever saw Annie's dad, but he liked him a lot.

Annie pulled away from her dad. 'How come you're back?' she asked excitedly.

'Been reassigned up north,' he replied. 'All this business at Spadeadam – you've probably read about it in the paper.'

Ben did his best not to catch Annie's eye. 'Yeah,'

she replied. 'Bits and pieces. Do you know what went on?'

James took a seat on Annie's bed and stretched his legs out. 'Not a clue, to be honest. It's all very mysterious. Some people seem to think it's a terrorist strike, and we've had certain intelligence—'

'What sort of intelligence?' Ben asked, a bit too quickly.

James looked slightly taken aback by his sudden question. 'I'm sorry, Ben,' he said quietly. 'It's the sort of thing I can't discuss.'

'No,' Ben muttered, slightly embarrassed. 'No, of course not.'

'Still,' James announced brightly, 'for what it's worth, I don't agree with them. Strikes me as being much more likely that it was an unexploded bomb left over from the war. Or something like that. Whatever it is, it's a mess. Anyway' – he smiled over at his daughter – 'it means I'm going to be around for a bit, I'm afraid.'

Annie grinned at him.

'Well,' James declared, standing up and stretching his legs, 'I'd better get back to it.' He made to leave. 'Oh,' he said, turning round just as his hand touched the doorknob, 'your mum said you went bird-watching in that area.'

Ben and Annie nodded mutely.

'See anything interesting?'

Ben blinked, his mind suddenly blank as he tried to think of something to say.

'Oh,' he managed finally, shrugging his shoulders as nonchalantly as he could and turning to look out of Annie's bedroom window, 'you know. This and that.'

Know the Facts

Fact

In the 1950s, the CIA initiated Project MKULTRA. Its purpose was to use scientific techniques to affect and control people's minds. According to an official CIA document, this included research into 'substances which will promote illogical thinking and impulsiveness to the point where the recipient would be discredited in public'.

It is not known if the British government carried out similar research, though some people think it likely.

Fact

In 2004, excavations for a secret missile silo were uncovered within the grounds of RAF Spadeadam. No official documents relating to the construction of these silos appear to exist.

Fact

RAF Spadeadam contains a number of sites of Special Scientific Interest, and the RAF is scrupulous about conserving the wildlife and habitats that exist within the base.

Fact

The hen harrier is one of the rarest birds in the United Kingdom. Evidence suggests that breeding hen harriers are being routinely killed and if nothing is done to reverse this trend, this beautiful bird risks becoming extinct, at least in England.

Author's Note

Ever since I was a boy, I have enjoyed hiking outdoors – not only appreciating the physical challenges involved, but also being aware of the local wildlife. I am particularly concerned with the conservation of our natural wild birds and animals, and especially where individual species are at threat of disappearing for ever unless they are actively protected.

The hen harrier bird is one such species. In 2004, a survey by the RSPB, Scottish Natural Heritage and other countryside agencies found only 749 nesting pairs in the UK, almost all of which were in Scotland. Only ten pairs were found in England and this year only fifteen successful nests have been confirmed. This is a pitifully low number, considering that the birds have legal protection, and I would very much like to see their numbers increase.

For further information on the hen harrier, the Royal Society for the Protection of Birds (RSPB) has information on how you can help to save this amazing bird of prey, as well as giving you information on other birds at risk. See www.rspb.org.uk for further information. And

www.rspb.org.uk/youth/join_in/wex.asp for details of their wildlife explorers club.

Outside the UK, you will almost certainly find your own national organization to help protect birds and wildlife in your area.

For further information on species at risk – insects, birds, animals or reptiles:

www.wwf.org
www.worldwildlife.org/endangered
www.wildlifeprotection.info

Chris Ryan

If you would like to know more about helping to conserve wildlife and birds, both in the UK and abroad, you can join the world's most exciting wildlife club for young people:

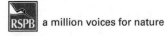 a million voices for nature

Be a Wildlife Explorer

Join the club for:

* a great membership pack, including posters
* a magazine, *BirdLife*, six times a year
* the chance to enter competitions and take part in activities and wildlife holidays
* and free entry to more than 100 RSPB nature reserves.

It's a great way to learn about wildlife and to help protect birds. There are family membership packages too, and teenagers can also become RSPB Phoenix members and get their own environmental magazine, *Wingbeat*, four times a year. Your membership will help conserve wildlife both in the UK and abroad.

Full information at:
www.rspb.org.uk/youth/join_in/wex.asp